D0539728

TIMECATCHER

04636330

TIMECATCHER

* * *

Marie-Louise Fitzpatrick

Orion
Children's Books

First published in Great Britain in 2010
by Orion Children's Books
a division of the Orion Publishing Group Ltd
Orion House
5 Upper St Martin's Lane
London WC2H 9EA
An Hachette UK company

1 3 5 7 9 10 8 6 4 2

Copyright © Marie-Louise Fitzpatrick

The right of Marie-Louise Fitzpatrick to be identified
as the author of this work has been asserted.

All rights reserved. No part of this publication may be
reproduced, stored in a retrieval system, or transmitted,
in any form or by any means, electronic, mechanical,
photocopying, recording or otherwise, without the prior
permission of Orion Children's Books.

A catalogue record for this book is
available from the British Library.

ISBN 978 1 84255 677 1

Typeset by Input Data Services Ltd,
Bridgwater, Somerset

Printed in Great Britain by Clays Ltd, St Ives plc

The Orion Publishing Group's policy is to use papers that
are natural, renewable and recyclable products made from
wood grown in sustainable forests. The logging and manufacturing
processes are expected to conform to the environmental
regulations of the country of origin.

www.orionbooks.co.uk

For Mam, with love,
and in memory of Cara –
my Duff.

I wish to acknowledge the invaluable support I have received from the Arts Council of Ireland.

For encouragement, time, eagle eyes and good advice, many thanks to Michael, Caroline, Kate, Mary, Niamh, Beth, Dylan, Diarmuid, Oliver, Eunice, and all at the old Brunswick Street Mill.

$* \! \text{\Large✳} \quad 1 \quad \text{\Large✳} \! *$

The day was hot, too hot for shopping. Jessie brushed her hair from her neck for the umpteenth time. The city smelled of tar and car exhaust with a trace of coffee and chips. At least they were on their way home now. Five more minutes and they'd turn onto Sitric Street and be at their own front door.

'Then fifteen minutes to walk Duff and ten to do my maths will make it five-thirty,' she calculated. She'd be just in time for her favourite TV programme.

Jessie switched the shopping bag from her right hand to her left; the handles were biting into her palms. Her mam was in front of her carrying two bags, both over-packed, so when she stopped suddenly Jessie trod on her heels and stuff fell all over the pavement. Jessie's mam turned with that look on her face, a look Jessie knew only too well. Drat! She's forgotten something.

'Aw, no, Mam. Please say you didn't forget something?'

Her mother pulled a face and nodded. 'The buttons. I forgot the buttons.'

'We've been out since school dragging around the shops, Mam. You said we'd be home by five. You promised.' Jessie picked up a loaf of bread and a parcel of lace then caught two spools of white thread as they rolled towards the gutter.

'I think we'll have to go back, Jessie love,' her mother was saying. 'I can't do without those buttons. I have to finish the dress tonight. The bride-to-be is coming to collect it tomorrow, first thing.' She dithered on the footpath, looking left and right, chewing a fingernail.

Jessie re-bagged the bits then threw her weight against a nearby wall and waited. Her mam was always in a twist about something or other. If it wasn't dress deadlines, it was zips. Or hem-lengths. Or what to have for dinner. Everything turned into a production; it drove Jessie nuts. Dad had been the calm one, the decision maker. Now, every day there was a drama. They would probably have to go back into town but by the time her mother finally made up her mind about it they'd have to run to catch the haberdashery before it closed. There went her TV programme.

'Whoa!' Jessie gasped and jumped away from the wall. Something had brushed ever so lightly across the top of her head. 'What was that?'

She looked up but nothing was there, just solid wall. Her scalp prickled. Fingers fluffing her hair, that's what it had felt like. She shivered and checked around her. Her mother was still droning on about buttons. She hadn't missed a beat, not even when Jessie squawked.

Jessie gazed up at the wall. The building appeared to be a big old mill. There were some windows, tiny ones, all far above her head. Too far away for fluffing fingers. To her left was an opening, an archway leading off the street. Some signs surrounded the archway, clustered hodge-podge on the wall.

'"Kickboxing Club, Opening Soon",' she read. '"The Grey Mill Studios" ... "The Dublin Button Factory".'

'Mam,' said Jessie.

'Maybe if I use hooks and eyes in the sleeves there'll be enough buttons in the box at home – no, that'll never work—'

'Mam,' said Jessie.

'No, it's no use, we'll just have to walk back into Henry Street right now. If we hurry we'll—'

'MAM!'

'There's no need to shout, Jessie Minahan, I'm standing right in front of you.' Mrs Minahan sounded rather hurt.

'"The Dublin Button Factory",' said Jessie.

'I beg your pardon?'

'"The Dublin Button Factory". It says it up there on the wall, on that sign. See?'

Jessie's mother looked up.

'A button factory! We've been here two months and no one's ever mentioned it. You'd think since I'm in the dress design business *someone* would have. Come on then, what are you waiting for?'

Mrs Minahan disappeared through the archway. Jessie rolled her eyes and followed.

The archway opened out into a square yard. Some cars were parked there, hugging the shadows, and the building rose up around them on all four sides. Two walls were grey and two were built of small red bricks, old worn bricks in dusty shades of pink-red, purplish and orange. There were a lot of doors and an odd assortment of windows dotted around. They were all painted blue, the kind of blue Jessie had painted skies when she was five.

Two metal stairways ran from the yard to the first floor. One was to Jessie's left, near the street entrance. The other was at the back of the yard, leading to a door with a sign that read 'The Dublin Button Factory'. Mrs Minahan was already rapping on that door. A young woman with blonde hair and huge brown eyes opened it. She was wearing a long pink skirt and a T-shirt with a crazy orange and pink design.

'Yez?' she said.

'Buttons,' said Mrs Minahan. 'I'm here for buttons. Small, white, pearl. Thirty-five. I'm in the middle of a wedding dress, up to my eyes. Just been in town, forgot the—'

'Buttons?' said the girl. 'Ah, yez, buttons. JAY-SON!' She yelled the name over her shoulder in an accent Jessie decided was Polish.

'Come in, come in.' The girl waved her arms vaguely at Mrs Minahan and threw a quick smile at Jessie.

The room was small. Strange-looking machines crowded the worktops and a big old-fashioned weighing scales squatted on the floor underneath. Pink paint peeled down the walls in large, hanging curls. A bashed filing cabinet lurched in one corner, spilling its contents at various angles and, beside it, a Belfast sink was piled with stained coffee cups. In the opposite corner a flight of four steps walked into a solid wall. Two desks jostled

4

for space in the middle of the room. One held a PC, the other a laptop, many assorted pens and a mound of paper.

But, best of all, there were buttons everywhere, thousands of them. They were heaped on the worktops and big drifts of them covered the floor, crunching under Jessie's feet.

'Sit, sit. Jason, he will be here in a minute, yez? He will explain about the buttons.'

Mrs Minahan sat. She eyed the piles of buttons around her feet with a puzzled frown. Jessie eyed the weird machines.

'What's that for?' she asked, pointing to one which had a miniature chimney coming out of it.

'Ah, Jason will tell you, Jason will explain. I only work here two months, yez?' The girl smiled quickly then rapped on the door behind her.

'Jason!'

Loud footsteps, the door swung open and a man burst through. He was tall, a little overweight, and had sandy hair which looked, Jessie thought, as if its owner spent a lot of time raking his fingers through it.

'Customers, Nat? Great! What can I do you for?' He grinned and cracked his knuckles.

Jessie craned her head to see around him into the other room. It was dark in there and she could just make out what seemed to be a heap of old clothes in the middle of the floor. Nat pulled the door shut with a snap.

'No, no. They are here for buttons, Jason. You will explain the button situation, please.'

'Look,' Mrs Minahan said, turning from Nat to Jason. 'I just want buttons, thirty-five small, white, pearl buttons. I'm a designer. Exclusive one-offs. I'm making a wedding dress. It has to be ready by tomorrow. Bride's last fitting before the big day, I'll be up all night finishing it. I just want thirty-five—'

'Small, white, pearl ones. Mmm.' said Jason, looking at the pile on the floor. 'Aha! There's one,' and he reached down and plunged his hand into one of the button mounds. 'Dunno if we'll find you *thirty-five* but we'll have a go.' He knelt down and began sifting through the mass on the floor. Jessie glanced at her mother and tried not to giggle.

'You know, if we *all* search we'll get there much faster.' Jason smiled at Mrs Minahan. 'You're looking at all that's left of the Dublin Button Factory, I'm afraid.' He waved his hands at the buttons on the floor. 'It closed down last year.'

Mrs Minahan became flustered. 'Well then, you should take down those signs outside. If it says buttons, people will expect buttons.'

'Well, as it happens, it suits us just fine as it is. In point of fact, you're the only person to call looking for buttons all year. Not many people want to buy loose buttons any more. Meanwhile the Button Factory provides us with the perfect disguise and disguises are part of our stock and trade, Mrs – er, em . . .'

'Minahan,' Mrs Minahan snapped. Jessie went slightly pink and watched Jason through her fringe.

'And what exactly is your stock and trade that it needs disguising?' Her mam's voice tightened.

6

'Detection,' said Jason. 'Aha. I detect *another* wee button, that's five.'

'I beg your pardon?'

'I am a private detective, Mrs Minahan,' said Jason. 'Welcome to the Button Detective Agency.'

✳✳ 2 ✳✳

Jessie Minahan's List of Cool Careers: number one – veterinarian, number two – archaeologist, number three – private investigator. The buttons bit circles into Jessie's palms and knees as she joined Jason's hunt on the floor but she was too busy asking questions to care. Thirty-five pearl buttons, plus four spare and a large bag of assorted later, she had a potted history of the Button Detective Agency and loads of inside information on how a detective operates.

As factories go, the Dublin Button Factory had been rather tiny but then buttons are tiny things. It had only taken three people to run the machines and everything had fitted into these two small rooms.

'We'll clean out this room eventually.' Nat waved her arms at the chaos. 'But we're too busy just now. We don't need loads of space.'

Jason had trained in computers and switched to investigative work when he saw a job advertised in the evening paper. It was eight months now since he had set up his own agency in the mill. Nat had joined him recently. (Natasha Moroshkin, Russian, not Polish.) A lot of their work was done by phone and Internet, and the rest by what Jason called 'good old-fashioned legwork'.

'Legwork —' Jason fished another pearl button out of a particularly deep pile '— actually involves an awful lot of sitting around. In cars waiting for people to leave buildings and in bars and hotel lobbies pretending to read newspapers.'

'And pretend shopping,' said Nat. 'And lots of standing around trying to look like wallpaper.'

For a moment Jessie tried to imagine what kind of wallpaper Nat would resemble and a glance at her mother told her she was thinking the same thing. The Russian girl was very pretty and it was hard not to think that she would stand out in any crowd.

Guessing what they were thinking, Jason laughed. 'Believe me, Nat can fade away into the background when she wants to. We have a whole heap of disguises: wigs, make-up, even a few false noses. One day I'm a businessman, the next a road sweeper. Nat might be a student or a tourist or an office worker out on her lunch break. Whatever allows us to find the person we are investigating and stay close, watching, making notes, taking photos. Eventually we get the information our client wants. Patience, that's what it's all about. Patience.'

'Ever investigated a murder?' Jessie asked excitedly. 'Or a big bank robbery?'

''Fraid not.' Jason laughed. 'Them's jobs for the boys in blue. We get the little jobs the Gardaí don't have time for; people's private wee secrets and mysteries. Marriage and money-matters, *that's* what we deal with. All very ordinary, really. Run-of-the-mill, geddit?'

Mrs Minahan laughed and Jessie and Nat groaned.

'But how do people know you're here?' Mrs Minahan asked.

'The Yellow Pages, the Internet, the small ads. People like the *anonymity* of this place.' Jason shrugged. 'Folk are funny about being seen going into a detective agency. What if they bumped into their Great Aunt Janey—'

'Where do those go?' Jessie pointed to the corner she'd noticed earlier where four steps ran up to a solid brick wall.

'Ah, the steps. Dunno. Like that when we got here.'

'But they can't just go nowhere,' said Jessie. 'There must have been a door there once.' She crunched across the buttons and sprang lightly up the steps, one, two, three, four.

'Nooooo!' Both Jason and Nat dived forward and grabbed her just as she reached the top. Jason swept her off the step and plonked her in front of Mrs Minahan.

'They are – how do you say? – insincere.' Nat smiled brightly.

'I beg your pardon?' Mrs Minahan looked as astonished as Jessie.

'Wobbly, instable—'

'Unstable! Yes, yes, that's right. Unreliable, even,' Jason said quickly. 'The steps are unstable. Very. Especially at this time of the year—' a frown from Nat '—the heat makes them swell. Not the best place to be dashing about. There could have been a nasty accident. So, have you enough buttons there, Mrs Minahan? Can we fill another bag? No? Glad to be rid of them, shame to just *throw* them out.' Jason started tugging on his knuckles again.

10

What's up with him? Jessie thought. Suddenly he was acting like one of those creepy TV gameshow hosts.

She looked back at the steps. His eyes followed hers anxiously. What is it? What's he afraid of? she thought. They're just ordinary steps.

Except they didn't go anywhere.

Mrs Minahan gathered up the shopping and button bags and started moving towards the door. 'Thanks so much for the buttons, Jason, it's very kind of you. Sorry for taking up so much of your time. Come on, Jessie. These people have work to do.'

Mrs Minahan was out the door and halfway down the stairs in a moment. Jessie was reluctantly turning to follow her when it happened; a large hank of her hair was grabbed and pulled. Sharply.

'Ow!' Jessie spun round and frowned at the two detectives who gawped at her in astonishment.

'Ha, ha, ha,' said a voice.

Jessie stared. There was a boy floating half-in, half-out of the wall, his face level with Jason's. He appeared to be lit from within and he was switching himself on and off like a Christmas tree. Jessie stood rooted to the spot, her mouth open in disbelief. She could feel the blood draining from her face. She blinked hard. The boy was still there. Jason and Nat were looking from the bizarre vision in the wall to Jessie and back again, alarmed expressions on their faces. Suddenly there was a whooshing sound like a giant vacuum cleaner and the blinking boy was sucked away into the bricks.

'Je-ess!' Mrs Minahan's voice sounded very far off, as if she was already leaving the yard.

Jessie gulped. She took a deep breath and opened her mouth to answer but Nat and Jason both quickly brought fingers to their lips and shook their heads frantically. She closed her mouth but it fell open again of its own accord.

'Please.' Jason whispered urgently. 'Don't tell your mam what you just saw. It's important.'

Jessie nodded uncertainly and moved towards the door.

'I won't,' she croaked, staring at the brick wall where the boy had been. 'But—' she faced Jason and said, as firmly as her chattering teeth would allow, 'I'll be back.'

✳✳ 3 ✳✳

𝓗e had been playing the car game, G had, when the woman and girl stopped in the street below him. The car game was his fallback for bad days, for when he had worn all his other games out, for the times when he felt like tearing around the building, screeching like a banshee. It wasn't much of a game but the counting calmed him. One point for every red car, two for black or white, four points for green, yellow or blue. Five for silver and gold, eight for a truck, ten for a bus. Fifteen for a motorbike. He'd always wanted to ride a motorbike. Death wasn't fair. Death was boring.

He'd just decided to keep going until he reached five hundred when they'd come along; the woman twittering on about wedding dresses and the girl looking rightly cheesed off. He seized his chance and lured them in with button bait.

Easy peasy.

There hadn't been anyone his own age in the mill since his accident, and that was years ago. A particularly dull day had just turned interesting.

G had played here with a gang of boys, once. Before the accident. The lock on the archway gates was broken and they would come after school to play on the huge scrapheap which filled the yard back then. Friends, the boys had been his friends, but when the accident had happened they had all run away. Left him alone and dying. Some friends!

Since then these rooms had been his home, his prison. As soon as he had turned ghost he tried to leave. He wanted to run down the street to his gran; she could make everything better again, he was sure of it. He'd tried strolling out through the gate, floating through a window, even running through the outside walls really, really fast – but the mill shrugged him straight back in, like some giant bouncy castle.

It had taken him a long time to accept that he was really dead.

A day or two later someone had padlocked the gates good and proper and his friends had never come back. G had waited for a whole week, watching the street from the walls. Sometimes he thought he recognised a face and called out a name; the kid would look about, then walk on. But G kept on watching, day after day, the boys messing and shoving, the girls whispering and shrieking.

On the seventh day G decided he was going to get someone's attention. He would use the big iron gates to stage a little exhibition. He'd push his face, legs and arms through the solid metal and recite Georgy-Porgy at the top of his voice, preferably as the largest group of giggling girls was passing by. He was going to make them screech and jump; it was going to be the best fun ever!

But just as he'd been about to begin, a strange thing happened. Everything froze. He couldn't move hand or foot; he couldn't even turn his head. Some unseen force held him suspended in midair. Suddenly it let him go and he tumbled backwards into the yard. He lay on the cobbles looking up as a huge ghost materialised above him. A big man with long grey hair, a beard and a menacing look in his eye.

'I'm Greenwood,' he growled. 'Master Greenwood to thee, boy. This is my place, see? Here, what I say goes.'

The big ghost's accent sounded English, and from the look of his dusty green clothes, he'd been dead a long time. He lowered his face towards G's and simultaneously made a gesture with his huge hands. G found himself rising four feet off the cement and hovering helplessly almost nose to nose with the other ghost.

'You live here, too?' G found his voice at last. 'How are you holding me in place? Is it a trick?'

'Never you mind how I'm doin' it,' the man growled. 'Just remember I can spend hours every day lockin' thee in one spot just like I'm doin' now, so mind what I say.' The man narrowed his eyes. 'Other spectres know they're not welcome here. If I could toss thee out, I would, but you're one of them ghosts that's tied fast to the place where they died so I'm stuck with thee. Well, just remember not to get on wrong side o' me; I can make thine every night and day a misery.'

He straightened up and lowered his hands. G plopped back onto the cement and cautiously floated himself back up onto his feet.

'What's thy name, boy?' demanded the big ghost.

15

That was the moment when G first realised he'd forgotten it. His name. He searched his memory frantically but . . . nothing. So he had said the first thing that came into his head.

'G. G for Ghostboy.'

Master Greenwood curled his lip. 'You're new to death, Ghostboy. You need to settle down, not be so noisy and giddy-some. There's some rules to bein' a ghost; be best if you keeps 'em.' He put his massive hands behind his back and began to pace across the yard. 'Rule one, no showin' thyself to the livin'. Rule two, no talkin' to the livin'. Rule three, no glowin' before midnight.' Greenwood stopped then and eyed the boy. 'I don't have much time for chit-chat and suchlike. You keep them rules and stay out o' my business and we should get by just fine.' And with that he had walked into a wall and disappeared.

Ghost stuff took a while to get used to, even the cool bits. Floating, not walking. Flying, not running. It took time to master lighting up at will and switching in and out of visible mode. Ghost sleep was a slow fade to black, no dreams. G had gone on playing his games alone, only catching the odd glimpse of the big ghost, never getting more than a grumped greeting. He had rattled around the old mill like a stone in a tin can. Well, he hadn't actually been able to rattle, more howl, growl and squawk.

Then, a year after he'd turned ghost, the mill's big gates had opened again and workmen came and began clearing and renovating. The button maker arrived and set up his factory right in the two rooms G knew Greenwood favoured most. The button man had kept his hissing, clanking machines in the room overlooking the yard and used the other for storage.

Artists had moved in too and turned rooms throughout the building into studios. G was having some fun again; a little light haunting here and there, nothing too flash, nothing too scary. He got up to some of his best tricks when Greenwood was holed up in the button rooms or out on some excursion or other. The rest of the mill was his then; that was the only time he could count on not being stopped mid-spook. And the artists made such easy targets.

Sometimes he would stand and watch them work, especially the good ones. He would watch them as they mixed colours and placed them on the canvas in layers of light and dark. But after a while his fingers always started to twitch. He was certain-sure he could do a better job than any of them if he only had the chance. How he wanted to grab the brush and paint the images that danced in his head! Then he'd step up behind the painter he was watching, his mouth just behind an ear, and softly say: 'Haaaa.' Some of them were used to it now but the new ones always jumped and dropped the brush or streaked it across the picture and then ran, shaking, to another room, to tell.

One night, shortly after the artists had moved in, G stared at a painting for so long he absent-mindedly reached for a brush and lifted it towards the canvas. As soon as he became aware of the paintbrush in his hand it slipped from his grasp and hit the floor and, try as he might, he couldn't pick it up again. In his frustration he lashed out at the table with its pots and jars and tubes. It had all gone smashing and crashing.

Suddenly Greenwood appeared, but instead of telling G off, he asked the boy how he had done it.

'Try again, lad. Lift the brush again.'

G had looked at the brushes scattered all over the studio floor and leaned down towards a particularly large one with a very satisfying broad handle. His hand shook a little as he reached for it. He closed his fingers around it and lifted. But his hand came up empty.

'Again, boy. Try again.' Greenwood's voice had been almost gentle, coaxing him.

'Since when are you Mister Friendly?' G's eyes narrowed. 'You leave me all on my own every day, hardly say a word to me, and now that I can do something you can't, you want to be my pal? What are you after?' G kicked out at a glass jar and it rolled a little way across the floor.

'Haa!' Another kick sent a paint tube flying. 'I'm going to have fun now, Master Greenwood, and you can't stop me. I'll turn this whole mill upside down. I'll—' and then G was frozen, mid-kick. Greenwood had him locked in place and the expression on his face turned sour and threatening. Now there were two new rules.

'No physical contact with the livin'.'

'No movin' objects in the presence of the livin'.'

'Two more rules to break when the Enemy isn't looking,' G had muttered at the wall when Greenwood finally released him and vanished.

Then last year the old button maker became ill and closed down his business and the detective guy had taken over the Button Factory rooms. He'd put a few computers into the front room and filled up the back room with all his other stuff. Greenwood had been very put out at first. Silly old codger, with his secrets and his rules! But less access to those rooms for Greenwood meant him spending more time in the rest of the building. And that made breaking the rules a little harder for G.

Well, today G had broken four rules in a row and it had been deadly! After he'd got the Jessie girl's attention and waited to see that she read the button sign, he'd left his perch high up in the wall beside the gateway, passed through a few rooms and stopped just behind the factory. Greenwood's rooms; enemy territory!

He hid in the bricks and watched the girl and her mother arrive at the office door, watched them rummage around the floor with the detectives for buttons. Then he'd waited until the mother left before popping out and giving it his all. The girl's face had been priceless but she hadn't gone all sissy and screeched. He wondered what she'd said when she finally got her voice back. Greenwood had pulled him through the wall just as she opened her mouth.

Blast him. It was humiliating. He had drawn G through the bricks as easily as a magnet pulls paperclips.

'You made a right mess today, Pooka-boy, and you are goin' to fix it,' Greenwood growled through clenched teeth. 'The girl will be back and when she comes, you'll be nice as pie. Then you're goin' to get rid o' her.'

Greenwood had spelled it out for him. He wasn't to scare her, there was to be no noise of any sort. G was to be dull, dull as a ditch. The girl had to be persuaded that the mill held nothing to interest her. Under no circumstances was G to mention Greenwood.

Why was this so important to Greenwood? Why was he making a fuss about some kid? What was so important about the Button Factory rooms? He was hiding something, he had to be. Not that G cared about that. He was only interested in Jessie.

'He thinks she'll be back. Well, when she comes, I'll be ready.'

Greenwood wanted her out of the mill; G wanted her in. It was a pity she was a girl but that couldn't be helped. A kid is a kid and G was tired of being alone. The big ghost had ordered him to get rid of her – well, he would. He'd do it his way, but.

And his way would mean the Jessie girl would be here to stay.

✳✳ 4 ✳✳

'There was a boy in the wall,' Jessie said to Duff. 'Really. In the old mill. A boy. A strange, laughing boy. I swear, Duff.'

Duff's brown eyes stared steadily at her. The little grey terrier was lying in her lap as she tackled her homework.

'What did I see, Duff? A trick of the light? No, light doesn't laugh and pull your hair. And the detectives saw him too, Duff. What was he? A ghost?'

There, she'd said it out loud. Ghost. She'd seen a ghost. She rolled the word around her head. Ghost, ghost, ghost. At approximately five-thirty pm today, she, Jessie Minahan, had seen a ghost. But she didn't believe in ghosts. Did she?

Duff sat up and licked her ear. He had enjoyed his walk but Jessie knew he'd still like to go and play outside.

'I have to do my homework, Duff.' But how was she supposed to concentrate?

Mrs Minahan's sewing machine putt-puttered in the kitchen downstairs. Jessie's bedroom here was smaller than in their old house in Kilkenny. Her mam had painted the walls the same shade of yellow but the sunlight didn't flood this room the way it had that other one. Duff moved off her knee and stuck his black nose

21

up against the windowpane, leaving a big wet splodge. He gave a little whine.

No one had gardens on Sitric Street. It was a cul-de-sac so all the kids played out on the street. From her window Jessie could see the boy from number four flying up and down on his skateboard and two girls swinging round and round on ropes hitched to lampposts. It was after eight so all the really little ones had gone in to bed. Some dolls and tricycles were still lying about on the path.

She finished another fraction but was pretty sure she'd got it wrong. Again. Joining a new school at the end of the school year had been a pain. She was way ahead in some subjects, especially history, her favourite, and way behind in others. Maths fell into the way-behind category. In September Jessie would be starting secondary school. Another change, more new faces.

This year had been all pain and changes. It had started with a knock on the door on an icy day in January. A Garda, solemn and kind, telling Jessie and her mam that Dad had been in an accident at work. That Dad was dead.

The house in Kilkenny was sold; Mam said she couldn't bear to live there any more without Dad. Mam's sister lent them her house in Dublin while she was off in Australia. She'd be gone a few years; time enough for Mrs Minahan to resurrect her career as a dress designer and get the family's finances back in order.

Now here they were in Stoneybatter. Leaving home had been hard, leaving her friends had been harder still.

The first week they'd moved in the local kids had called every day asking for Jessie and Duff to come out. They were all younger than Jessie so the next week they had just asked for Duff, but Duff wouldn't go out without Jessie so they stopped calling altogether. Making friends didn't come easy to Jessie. Girls always thought she was snooty and a know-it-all, until they'd had a bit more time to get to know her. Boys weren't so quick to write her off.

She'd had good friends in Kilkenny. They spent last summer hanging out at the local swimming pool. Here, summer stretched away into the distance with nothing much to do.

Until now.

Now there was all this incredible stuff to find out. Who was the blinking boy in the wall of the old Stoneybatter mill? Was he a ghost or a magic trick? She wasn't sure about ghosts, but she definitely didn't believe in magic.

What were the detectives hiding? They had asked her not to tell her mam what she'd seen. Fine. But they were going to have to explain it to her.

Jessie chewed the top of her pen. 'And then there were the steps that went nowhere. They made such a fuss about them, the detectives. One minute they were all friendly and normal, next thing they can't get us out of there fast enough. Those steps weren't unstable; they were solid stone. And there were only four of them; if I had fallen I wouldn't have gone very far. And I said I'd go back, I told them so. When, Duffer? When do I go back?'

23

The dog put his head on one side as if considering her question.

A mystery. There was a mystery in the mill and maybe she could solve it. Jessie Minahan, private eye, investigates the Button Detective Agency and the boy in the wall. She shivered and curled her arms around herself. Duff settled down on the duvet and rested his head on her knee.

'Tomorrow? After school?'

Duff cocked an ear and wagged his stumpy tail.

'I'll bring you with me, Duff. That's it. I'll get you straight after school and we'll go for a walk. To the mill.' Just thinking about going back there made her heart thump faster. She'd feel braver with Duff along.

'You and me forever, Duff-dog.'

The little dog began to snore.

✳✱ 5 ✱✱

The next day, Friday, was even hotter. The classroom had been like an oven but the entrance archway of the mill was dark and cool. From it Jessie could see the Button Detective Agency door with the little sign which read 'The Dublin Button Factory' in old-fashioned letters.

What if they tell me I imagined him? she thought. What if they lie and pretend like nothing happened?

After all, from what they told her yesterday, lying and pretending was exactly what detectives did all day. At her feet Duff was getting impatient. He looked up as if to say, Which way? Left? Right? Into the yard? Out? When Jessie still didn't move he peed against the wall and trotted on in to sniff around.

'He yours?'

And there was the boy. Just his face, in the wall, near hers. She could see his eyes and nose and mouth and, through them, the red bricks. A see-through black fringe flopped down over his dark eyes. Goosebumps crept slowly along Jessie's arms. Her heart started hammering and her breathing went funny.

'Yes, he's mine.' Jessie cleared her throat. 'He's called Duff.'

'Why?' asked the boy.

'When we got him he had a broken leg. My dad said it was a duff leg, so we called him that. Duff.'

'I'm G,' said the boy. 'G for Ghostboy.' He disappeared for a moment as a woman passed by on the street with a buggy and two small kids.

'What's your real name?' Jessie asked when the woman was gone.

'Dunno.'

'You don't know your real name?'

'Don't remember.' He shrugged. 'I've forgotten lots of stuff.'

'Well, your name is a pretty basic fact.'

'Banged my head when I died, didn't I?' He pulled his fringe back to show a deep gash on one side of his forehead. Jessie tried not to pull a face.

'That's where I died. I remember that.' The boy pointed to a place in the yard, over on the right, where the concrete was dipped and cracked.

Jessie's stomach did a flip. She considered asking how he died but it seemed impolite. The boy wasn't so squeamish.

'Ahhh! Splat!' He threw himself on the ground at Jessie's feet, his arms wide, head on one side, his tongue stuck out and eyes crossed. She laughed nervously. The boy's fringe had fallen back from his forehead and the gash on his forehead gaped. There were marks on the shoulder of his white T-shirt that looked like bloodstains.

Duff growled.

'It's all right, Duff. It's okay.' Jessie put her hand to the dog's collar and pulled him back a little from the boy. She could feel her hand shaking against Duff's neck.

'He's never seen a ghost before,' she said, trying not to let her voice quiver.

'How do you know he hasn't?' The boy laughed, floated upright and disappeared. He reappeared behind Jessie on the metal stairs, the ones that led up to a door marked 'The Grey Mill Studios'.

'Come on then,' said the boy. 'Let me bring you 'round.' And he swooped up the stairs, threading himself in and out of the steps, showing off. He passed through the door at the top and vanished again.

Jessie hesitated. Scared, excited, scared, excited; both at the same time. It was making her dizzy. She climbed the stairs slowly.

Duff gave a low woof and jumped after her. Jessie pushed open the door and found herself in a corridor. On one side of it there were windows facing onto the yard and on the other side there were doors with numbers on them. The corridor was dark after the bright sunlight outside. She blinked.

Her teeth clattered together. She twisted the edge of her T-shirt around one hand. Duff was standing tight against her legs. There was no sign of the boy.

'G?'

'Abracadabra!' He appeared from the ceiling above her, dangling upside-down like a trapeze artist. Duff sprang upwards, snapping air. G laughed and Jessie smiled nervously.

'Come on!' G righted himself and floated around the corner into another corridor full of doors and windows.

This one looked straight across the yard to the Detective Agency.

'What's behind the doors?' Jessie asked.

'Artists.' G stuck his nose up in the air and struck a pose, one arm on a hip, the other wielding an imaginary paintbrush.

Jessie choked back a giggle. 'Won't they hear us?'

'Not them,' said G. 'Half of them aren't in yet; they don't even get up till lunchtime. The others will either be painting like crazy—' he mimed big, dashing paint strokes '—or all upset 'cause they have artists' block. "I'll never paint again, I'll never paint again, I'LL NEVER PAINT AGAIN!"' he shrieked.

'Shush, they *will* hear you.' Jessie pulled herself back to the wall, expecting doors to fly open, left and right.

'Oh, don't worry, they won't come out,' G said airily. 'They know it's me, and they're even more scared of me than artists' block. Ha ha!'

Jessie blinked.

'You're not scared of me, but?' he grinned.

She shook her head. She still felt a little scared but she wasn't about to admit it.

He moved on down the corridor and she followed. Suddenly she felt as if she was upstairs in a dolls' house, with the front taken off. Beside her a huge door had been slid open along runners, leaving a big yawning hole and a long drop to the ground.

'They open it in this weather to keep the place cool,' said G and promptly walked straight out through it and fell. 'Whaaaaa!' Jessie laughed and went nearer to the edge to look for him.

'Boo!' He popped up just in front of her. She jumped.

She looked down at the yard far below and shivered. 'Why is there a door here? What's it for?'

'Dunno,' said G. He swooped back into the building and stood behind Jessie. 'This was a flourmill, once. Something to do with shifting sacks of flour, maybe?'

Jessie made to step back from the opening.

'Look at that,' said G, pointing across the yard to the room under the Detective Agency. 'That's going to be a kick-boxing club. Hi-*ya*! Hi-*ya*! Hi-*ya*!' Suddenly he began to karate chop the air around Jessie's head and high-kick towards her face. She tried to stop herself from backing away and clutched at the wall. Ghost hands couldn't hurt her. Could they? She heard his hands and feet whistling as they flew through the air. Too close. Way too close. Duff was snarling.

'Please don't do that—' Jessie began.

'Hi-*ya*!' His hand sliced past her ear. Surely her hair had moved that time? She glanced down at the yard again. Her heels were backed up right against the edge of the ledge. The sweat on her palms was making her lose her grip on the wall.

Idiot, she thought. He's a ghost, just walk through him.

Too late.

'HI-*YA*!' G yelled and lunged towards her. Duff jumped forward, trying to bite at the scentless shadow that seemed to be attacking Jessie but there was nothing to get his teeth into and he went straight through. Jessie felt a hand make contact sharply with her shoulder and then she was falling backwards, clutching at air. The sky loomed above her; for a few heart-stopping seconds she stopped breathing from sheer terror. Then something grabbed and pulled her, and she was back inside, landing in a heap on the dusty cement floor. Duff was dancing about her, snapping and snarling at G, who was hovering just outside the opening making faces. She grabbed Duff's collar and faced the boy, her terror turning to anger.

'What did you do that for? I nearly fell. You nearly made me fall.' Jessie was shouting. She didn't care who heard her. She saw Jason and Nat's faces appear at the top of a window on the opposite side of the yard. They both looked horrified; they must have seen what happened. Well, she wouldn't be here now if they hadn't hustled her out yesterday without an explanation. She glared at them.

'Z'only messin'.' G was clicking his fingers and disappearing and reappearing to the beat. His fingers made no sound so he made the noise with his tongue. Click, click, click.

'Stop doing that!' snapped Jessie, standing up, still with one hand on Duff's collar.

G floated into the corridor and let his fringe fall over his eyes. He stayed visible but went on soundlessly finger-clicking.

'You're such a girl!' he complained. 'You're all right, aren't you? What are you making a fuss about? I wasn't really going to let you fall. Knew I could grab you back in. Probably.'

'Probably? You pushed me out that door on the *off-chance* you'd be able to pull me back in again?'

G mumbled something and shoved his ghost hands inside the pockets of his black jeans. Jessie turned away angrily and started back towards the stairs, dragging the furious Duff with her. When she got there G was standing at the exit door, barring her way.

''M sorry.'

'Yeah, right.' Jessie picked up Duff and shook her hair away from her face. 'Get out of my way.'

'Don't go.'

She took a deep breath, stepped forward and walked through him.

He turned in the doorway. 'The other ghost, he said I had to make you go away,' he said sulkily.

Jessie wobbled on a step for a second then resumed stomping downwards. Duff was heavy in her arms and her knees were trembling. She needed to concentrate on getting down the stairs.

'Greenwood, the other ghost, he has a secret. Something about the mill, something to do with the button rooms, so he doesn't want you hanging around.'

Jessie reached the bottom step and put Duff down. Breathe, she told herself. Keep breathing.

'The detectives are in on it.'

Jessie straightened up. She was determined not to give the boy the satisfaction of looking back up at him. Instead she paused and looked to her right, the exit to the street and the way home. To her left was the other stairway, the one leading up to the detectives' offices.

Right. The way home. Home to Mam and the sofa and her favourite TV programme.

Left. The stairs to the detectives' office. She had questions, they had the answers.

Right or left?

No contest.

She turned left.

✳ ✳ 6 ✳ ✳

The mug of tea Nat gave Jessie didn't do much to calm her down. There was a squeak in her voice now as she pulled a face and said, 'This tea is full of sugar.'

'Yez!' Nat nodded her head vigorously. 'Good for shock.'

Jessie's stomach lurched. Yuck! Sugar-coated teeth, just what she needed.

'Here, I'll have it,' said Jason. 'My nerves are fairly jangled as well. I'll make you a fresh one.' He took the mug from Jessie and pulled out the teabags again.

'G, he calls himself G,' said Jessie.

'Em, really? Interesting,' said Jason. 'We wouldn't know, of course. Never laid eyes on him till yesterday. Did we, Nat?'

'Yez, never.' Nat nodded again, staring anxiously at Jessie.

'You'd never seen him before?' Jessie's voice wavered. Were they being level with her?

Jason smiled and handed her a new mug of tea. 'We've heard about him all right. Apparently he pops up every now and then; some of the artists have spotted him. But I'd never actually seen him myself before yesterday. Not personally.'

33

Lying and pretending?

'Right. I see.' Jessie narrowed her eyes. 'What about the other ghost, then?'

'Other ghost?'

'The boy, he said there was another one.'

'Oh, you wouldn't want to mind what he says. He's an awful liar. Always telling stories. Right little pest.'

'How do you know that if you've never seen him before?'

Jessie waited. Jason shrugged and buried his face in his tea.

'You said he only turns up now and then.'

'Well, that's it exactly. He turns up occasionally, causes all sorts of trouble, then disappears for ages. Only one or two sightings a year, I think. And thank goodness for that, I say!' Another smile. It didn't quite reach his eyes.

Lying, definitely.

Jessie carefully put her tea down among the buttons.

'I saw a ghost yesterday here in that wall,' she said firmly, pointing at the bricks. 'We all did. I saw him again today. He nearly killed me. I want to know what's going on. I want to know who Ghostboy is. I want to know who Greenwood is. I want to know ... I want to know where those four steps go.' She pointed to the corner.

Nat and Jason exchanged glances. Jason put down his mug.

'It's like this, young Jessie, there's nothing to tell. Nothing at all.'

'And if there was, we couldn't tell you anyway.' Nat shook her head sorrowfully.

Jessie glared at them. 'I nearly fell through that stupid door-thing. I could be lying out there right now with my brains splattered all over the yard.'

'Oh, I think we'd have cleaned you away by now.' Jason attempted another smile.

They'd say anything to make her leave, Jessie realised. They didn't care if she believed them, just so long as she went away and didn't come back. She would never know what was going on. She couldn't make them tell her.

Or could she? Did she have the nerve to try a bit of lying and pretending herself? She set her mouth in a grim line.

'I'll call the Press. I'll call the TV. I'll call the radio – the Gerry Ryan Show loves this kind of thing.'

'They won't believe you.' Jason folded his arms. He considered the floorboards for a moment then straightened up to his full height. 'You're a nice kid, Jessie, and we're sorry about what happened with the ghost boy, but if you bring the Press or TV here we'll make you look like a little fool. We'll say you're an attention-seeking, irritating little brat who insists on hanging around where she's not wanted.' Jason held Jessie's eye as her mouth fell open, this time in shock. She looked at Nat. The Russian girl bit her lip and nodded.

That was that, then. Jessie stood up and clicked her tongue. Duff trotted over to her. She walked slowly to the door then glanced back at the two detectives.

'You know—' she raised one eyebrow very deliberately '—I think I'll take my chances. You can say what you like to the Press but if G turns up they'll have no problem believing me, will they?'

Nat drew breath sharply; Jason's face changed colour.

'He wouldn't – he won't – he can't—'

They seemed to be trying to convince themselves rather then her.

'You think?' Jessie shrugged. 'He's a right show-off, him. Can you imagine what he'll do if a load of photographers and TV cameras arrive in the yard? Whoa! He'll put on some show, whizzing in and out of the walls, blinking like a demented traffic light! It'll be really cool!' She threw Jason back one of his false smiles. 'So. We'll be going then. Come on, Duff.' She made a show of reaching for the door handle.

'Wait!' Jason sighed. Jessie turned back into the room.

There was a ripple of wind and it suddenly felt a little chill, as if someone had opened windows on a cold day. The wall was quivering and shifting. Jessie backed into the door, really groping for the handle now. Duff whined and flattened himself onto the floor. A shadow moved through the wall and billowed towards them. As she gaped it resolved itself into the figure of a man, a big man. He was as wide as a wardrobe and so tall the light bulb passed through his head as he crossed the room. His grey hair straggled to his shoulders and a beard half-covered his face. He wore a faded green jerkin over faded green leggings.

He regarded Jessie solemnly and bowed. A giggle caught in her throat even as her legs turned to jelly.

She'd read about people laughing when in shock. She coughed and the giggle evaporated.

'Jessie, this is Master Greenwood.' Jason stepped forward, looking from girl to ghost. 'Master Greenwood, Jessie Minahan.'

* * 7 * *

Master Greenwood stood looking down at her, his fists on his hips. His features began to twist into a scowl and Jessie froze as his face came towards hers. Suddenly Duff erupted from behind her, his teeth stripped, snarling a snarl she had never heard before. The little dog was clearly terrified but meant to stand his ground between his mistress and this menace.

Greenwood blinked in surprise.

'Thy dog thinks you're worth takin' a risk for, Jessie Minahan.' Greenwood stared into Jessie's eyes. She tried to hold his gaze but couldn't. He seemed to see through her mind as easily as she could see the buttons through his feet. The ghost straightened up and scratched at his beard, frowning as he considered the growling dog. Jessie put a hand to Duff's back to reassure him but her palm was clammy and it shook. He growled louder.

'Well, hound,' Greenwood said softly. 'If you'll take a risk for her maybe I'll take a risk on her.'

Jessie looked up.

'Dogs know humans.' The ghost's expression had become less stern. 'They've got good instincts for who they can rely on and who'll kick them first chance they get. I'll let this hound's growl vouch for thee, Jessie Minahan. Don't seem to have much choice.'

38

Nat smiled and motioned Jessie towards a chair. Jason leant back against the bench and breathed out long and low. Greenwood moved back to the far wall. Duff barked once, then lay down in front of Jessie and kept an anxious eye on the large floating shape.

Then: 'What I tells thee now must never be told to another soul, not dead nor livin'; do you heed me, Jessie Minahan?'

'I– I– yes, sure, okay,' said Jessie. But she wasn't sure. How could she be? She was about to be told who-knew-what by a big green-grey ghost. Did promises to dead people even count? Another giggle threatened. She swallowed hard.

''Tis important, girl! The very turn o' time itself could depend on it.' He leaned forward. 'This knowledge comes with a price, lassie. You wants to know it and I'm goin' to tell it thee. Will you keep it secret, Jessie Minahan?'

Jessie felt her face flush. She had no idea what he was talking about, but she got to her feet and cleared her throat.

'I will, Master Greenwood.'

'Upon thy word of honour?'

'U–upon my word of honour.'

Greenwood floated to the window and looked out into the yard. Jessie sat back on her chair and Jason and Nat settled into theirs.

'I came to Dublin – Dublinia they called it then – in the year 1201. I was on the run, wanted in England for a bit o' thievin'. I had a price on my head and I meant

39

to lay low here a while till it was all forgot, and I could go home again.

'Back then Dublinia was a walled town all to one side o' river. 'Twas run by a man appointed by the King o' England so I deemed it prudent to live on t'other bank, in the little village o' Stoneybatter, where there were cows and trees and a grand little inn what brewed a nice ale. The King's justiciar rarely crossed the river and a man could live quiet-like, away from stink o' town. I had it good for a while, so good I let my guard down.

'In my time most men carried bows for huntin' and I carried a longbow, a type not seen much here in Ireland. Back home few could match my skill with it; I could shoot truer and farther than most. Now, I knew if the justiciar had heard tell o' me at all, he'd have heard I was a big man that carried a longbow and knew how to use it, so I was careful never to let village folk see me huntin'. I always carried my bow awkward-like; I acted clumsy. I let on that any game I killed was more by luck than skill.

'Then came eve o' the longest day o' year, a night for feastin' and dancin'. I stuffed myself full o' hog and cheese, I downed too many cups. I forgot where I was. When the villagers set up a contest to see who could shoot an arrow farthest, I stepped forward like a fool and drew my bow. The arrow flew high and straight and long. It flew a full eleven score and seven yards. The villagers had never seen the like before. They all cheered 'n' whooped at first but then they fell to talkin' and whisperin' and pointin'. I was that full o' ale I paid no mind and fell asleep in a ditch.

'Next mornin' I woke early and I could hear hounds bayin' in the distance. I realised what I had done; those hounds were after me. Seemed like a good time to run and hide, so I hauled myself out o' ditch and made for the trees. Now, hidin' someone o' my size may not seem easy and, anyways, the hounds would surely sniff me out.' Greenwood swung around from the window suddenly and looked at Jessie. 'Is that what you're thinkin', Jessie Minahan?'

Jessie nodded.

'But I am a man o' the forest, born among trees. And the trees around Stoneybatter were oaks and oak trees are full o' magic.'

'Magic?' Jessie blinked. Magic?

'Aye. 'Tis there if you knows how to use it.' Greenwood's eyes had a faraway look again. 'My grand-dame taught me the magic o' the trees when I was a bairn. Many's the time I'd used her tricks to hide from soldiers and dogs, so I searched around now for a likely tree, the older the better. One tree stood out from the rest; she was ancient and gnarled and huge. I climbed her right quick, got myself high up into her branches. I could feel she was a strong one; her power crept around me as I chanted the rhyme my grandmother taught me.

'"*Oak to man, man to oak. Leaf to hand, hand to leaf. Branch to arm, arm to branch. Green sap to red blood, red blood to green sap.*"'

'The words asked the tree to hide me, to charm the senses o' the passers-by so that all they'd see were leaves, all they'd hear was wind and all they'd smell was leaf and earth.

'I had no reason to think 'twouldn't work till a strange silence fell around me and the oak began to tremble. Suddenly I remembered that those were English words spelled for English oak, and I was not in England. The magic I sensed within the tree was not the magic I'd grown up with.'

He shook his head as if he still couldn't believe his stupidity and his grey hair floated around his face. 'I'd been in such a rush to hide myself I hadn't stopped to think how my grand-dame's spell would fall in these woods. And, worse still, 'twas the longest day, the summer solstice, the day when all magic is at its strongest. Suddenly, the air in front of my face was quiverin'. I reached my hand out towards it and my fingers vanished in front o' my eyes.' His voice dropped to a whisper. 'My little spell had ripped a hole in the very air.'

Jessie gasped and waited, her heart thumping.

'I plunged my head and shoulders in to see what was on t'other side.' He was speaking quickly now, his hands flying about him, acting out his words. ''Twas all swirlin' light and spinnin' dark. And there was magic at the bottom o' it. I could feel it race and shimmer across my skin, tuggin' me inwards. I could tell the magic was old, very old, and very strong, but I couldn't sense if it was bad or good. 'Twas just *there*, powerful and hidden, waitin' for someone practised enough to use it. Or someone fool enough to disturb it. I pulled my head back out o' that hole I'd torn before the magic could pull me in. I heard hounds again. Close. And the search party crashin' through trees.

42

'I tried sayin' the hidin' spell backwards, I tried a healin' spell. Nothin' happened.' He was shouting now, angry with himself still. Jessie shrank down on her seat. 'I'd made this mess and I couldn't fix it. I'd exposed this powerful magic thing; I could feel magic leakin' out into air around me. Any minute men would be climbin' the tree to fetch me down. The dogs were already at foot o' trunk, barkin' at me. Only thing I could think to do was give myself up so they wouldn't find this gash I had torn in the air. I couldn't heal it so I had to hide it.

'And that's what I did.'

He lowered his voice and struggled to compose his features. His eyes grew dark and distant.

'I was dragged off to the town jail, tried and sentenced to hang. Within a fortnight I was back in Stoneybatter, standin' on the gallows waitin' to die.

'In those last minutes I tried to think o' home, o' the forest I grew up in, but all I could think o' was the hole in the air amongst the branches o' that oak nearby. I kept thinkin' o' the magic that was leakin' out and the folk what might blunder in.

'"'Tis all my doin' and I've got to mend it." Those were my last thoughts before the hangman put the rope around my neck. The trapdoor 'neath my feet opened. I fell down.'

✳ ✳ 8 ✳ ✳

'There was another thief hanged that day.' Greenwood rubbed his neck absently.

Jessie glanced at Jason and Nat. They had obviously heard his story before, still they hung on his every word.

'I was just gettin' over the shock o' findin' myself a shade, floatin' above the crowd when, next thing, I have company.' Greenwood turned back into the room. '"A merry jig they're makin' me dance and not a fiddler in sight," says a voice in my ear. There beside me was another shade. I took a look at him and a look down at the gallows where his body was hangin' beside mine. 'Twasn't right, 'twasn't right at all.' Greenwood seemed to lose his train of thought.

'What do you mean, Master Greenwood?' Jessie ventured, not sure if she should speak.

'He wasn't full dead. His spirit was floatin' beside me but 'twas a full minute more before his body went still on end o' rope.'

'Eeeeew!' Jessie scrunched up her face in horror. 'Does everyone become a ghost when they die, then?'

'No. Only those with unfinished business here, or those who just aren't ready to move on.

'Anyways, there we were. Me and Sullivan Ellz'mede – that was his name – floatin' in air, and me wantin' to go back to the oaks to check the damage I'd done. Sullivan wanted to go hauntin'. He had a few scores to settle, had Sully. He wanted me to go too, for the sport, but scarin' folks is not my idea o' fun, so he went his way and I went back to the oaks. There was nothin' there.'

'Nothing?'

'Nothin' but trees. I couldn't find the hole I'd tore. 'Twere mended, or so I thought. I stayed in the forest, checkin' every now and then, particularly whenever the longest day came around. And seven years later I found it open again, the air all a-quiver, just like when I tore it first.'

'What did you do?'

'I was thinkin' on it when along came Sully.'

'What did he want?'

'Sully had been keepin' an eye on me all the time, see? Watchin' me for seven years to find out what I was watchin'. Curiouser than a ferret be Sully and he was through that openin' as quick as a ferret down a rabbit hole.'

'What did you do?'

'I went in after him. Had to make sure he did no mischief, because if there's mischief to be made, Sully will make it.'

'What was it like? What was in there, Master Greenwood?' Jessie leaned forward in her chair.

'That first time, 'twas like bein' a bairn again.' He smiled at the memory. 'I could hear Sully squawkin' and hootin' somewhere in the distance, then I was sucked in. I went spinnin' and tumblin' down, down,

down. Next thing, I'm back in branches o' the tree, only 'tis younger and straighter. I hear voices and I floats after them. There are folk, talkin' strange and wearing clothes from older days. I call out to them but they don't seem to see me or hear me, just go about their business, same as I'm not there. I spend a bit o' time lookin' around and then I go back to the tree. Next thing I'm spinnin' again; up this time, like a boat caught in the tide. It spits me out, back where I started, on the same day as I went in.'

'It's a time machine?' Jessie practically bounced on her seat, looking from Greenwood to Nat and Jason. 'You can travel through time and meet people who are dead and talk to them?'

Jason shook his head. 'Master Greenwood wasn't actually travelling *through* time, just watching a replay of it, if you know what I mean,' he said.

'Not really,' Jessie said, confused.

'I calls it the Timecatcher,' said Greenwood. ''Tis full o' shadows o' days, a shadow day for every day that's been, from long ago to yesterday.'

'All the shadow days are wrapped around each other and whirling constantly in circles, forming a giant vortex,' explained Jason, looking to Greenwood for confirmation. 'It seems that when you enter it you sort of slip between the layers and fall into a replay of one particular day out of the thousands. You can't interact with the people, in the same way you can't interact with actors in a film. They aren't really there. That's why Master Greenwood calls the days shadow days.'

'So you can't change things that have happened?'

Disappointment made Jessie's voice come out sulky.

'No. In fact, it's very likely people can't go in there at all, Jessie,' Jason said. 'You'd have to be able to fly to negotiate the vortex. Possibly only ghosts can travel safely in it.'

'I see.' Jessie tried to look impressed. This Timecatcher thing sounded amazing but sort of pointless. Under the bench the darkness shifted and caught her eye.

Greenwood looked at her thoughtfully. ''Twere hard for me to understand it when I first found it. What does it do? What is it for? Years o' explorin' the Timecatcher have given me some answers.'

Jessie tore her gaze away from the bench and tried to concentrate.

'The portal I ripped in the air opens for three days every seven years. Why? I'm not sure, but three and seven are magical numbers, that I know.' He paused, considered it a moment, then sighed. 'I've never worked that one out. Anyways, whenever the portal is open I spend every moment I can in there searchin'. Something inside that vortex is drawin' time towards itself, catchin' shadows o' days and hidin' inside them. Every dawn there's a new layer wrapped around the vortex; I've seen that with my own eyes. Then there's the oak.

'The oak is where I opened the portal, the oak is where I first felt the magic o' the source. When you travel through the vortex you land back in time but the first stop is always the hollow oak, or the spot where it used to stand. Everything starts and ends with that oak tree, so I believe that's where the power source is hidden. Right here, under this buildin'.' His eyes turned to the wall above the four stone steps.

Jessie caught her breath. 'Here? This is where the oak was? This is where you opened the portal?'

Greenwood was staring at the steps, lost in his thoughts again. Behind his back Nat nodded.

'But what does he mean when he says "the source"?' Jessie whispered to Nat and Jason.

'Let's put it at its simplest.' Jason raked a hand through his hair until it stood on end. 'Master Greenwood believes there is a magical object, a source of great power, and that it has created the Timecatcher.'

'What makes him believe that?'

'Because I can feel it!' Greenwood swung around to face her. ''Tis there, pulsing beneath everythin' inside the Timecatcher. 'Tis it created the vortex, 'tis it spins the days, 'tis it catches time. There has to be a source, somethin' solid, somethin' all that magic is stored in. In the old days folks with magical powers often drew magic into an object and stored it there.'

'What sort of object?' asked Jessie.

'Couple o' hundred years back I asked a young 'un to help me find out. A girl same age as you. Taney had special gifts, she could see things other folk couldn't, and I told her about the Timecatcher. She could sense the power like I could. She said in her mind she saw a ring, a powerful ring. But then, later, she seemed to have doubts. She promised me she'd tell me all she knew when she had it figured out but then she ran off and I never saw her again.' He frowned as if the girl's actions

48

still puzzled him. 'So, a ring, maybe, or a stone, a bowl, a sword.'

'But why can't you just see it, if it's in the tree?'

Greenwood struggled to find the right words. 'It only exists in one single day, one out o' thousands. There's only one single day where the power source is a real object that can be touched and picked up and moved.'

'The other days are a smokescreen,' explained Nat. 'Like hiding wood amongst trees, or the pebble on the stony beaches.'

'So the magical thing, the power source, can only be accessed if you find the right day?' Jessie ventured. 'You're sure?'

'As sure as I can be,' Greenwood said. 'I believe that, and Taney believed it too.'

'It's most likely hiding in the actual day it arrived there, at the oak,' Jason said.

'Wow!' Jessie's eyes were like saucers now.

'Old powerful magic, just layin' there and no one usin' it. If someone finds it and figures out how to use it, who knows what they could do? I've spent all my ghostdays tryin' to find a way to close that portal, permanent-like.'

'Master Greenwood believes that if he can find out *what* the power source is and what sort of magic created it, he can work out how to seal the portal,' Jason said. He fidgeted with his mobile phone. 'What do you think would happen if someone managed to move the power source, Master Greenwood? If they stole it?'

Greenwood ran his hand over his beard. 'The power source has been there maybe thousands o' years. No way o' knowin' how intertwined 'tis with this place, with the whole city.'

'What do you mean?' Nat sat forward on her chair. Jessie held her breath.

'The shadow days are there to hide the power source; it draws them to it like a cloak. But why not hide itself in layers of fog? Surround itself with shadows o' monsters, dragons and such? It has chosen to hide inside time, so the days must be important in some other way. Like the city and its past and future is somehow linked to the source.'

'So if someone moves the source—' Nat said slowly.

'Time moves too?' Jessie said, confused again.

Greenwood nodded.

'The power source, time, the city, they are all woven together somehow,' Jason ventured, 'so if someone disturbs the power source—'

'They disturb time,' finished Greenwood.

'What do you mean?' Jessie's voice shook. He couldn't mean what she thought he meant. Could he?

'Time may shift, here in the real world.' Greenwood said. 'The past could come tumblin' out o' Timecatcher and infect the present. If time shifts it could change history, change lives, change everything.'

'But what about the other ghost, Sullivan Ellz'mede? What happened to him?' asked Jessie.

'Harrumph!' Greenwood floated back to the window. 'He thought 'twas all a lark, a game; 'tis lucky the portal to the Timecatcher only opens for three days every seven years or he'd have had half the ghosts o' Dublin in it, like 'twas some old pantomime or a fancy playhouse. For him, 'twas entertainment. Me, I saw 'twas dangerous.'

The shadows under the bench shifted again. Something there? Jessie blinked and shook her head. No, nothing.

Greenwood turned back towards Jessie. 'One year I let myself get shut inside the Timecatcher and spent the next seven years searchin' it for the source o' power.' His face grew dark and strained. 'Right near lost my mind. The magic in there leaks into everything it touches. When I came back out I could feel that some o' that power were in me. Sure enough, next time Sully Ellz'mede is larkin' about, I raised a hand to quiet him and he couldn't move an inch; not till I let him. I could fix him in place for as long as I choose and he could do nothin' about it. It proved right useful keeping him out o' the Timecatcher and him rarin' to get in there again after he sees the power it gave me.

'Every seven years after that I held him in place when the Timecatcher was open and didn't let him go till I was good and sure the portal was closed again. But one year he got away from me just as it shut, flitted into Timecatcher, and was gone.' Greenwood grimaced and kicked out at the wall.

An inky shadow detached itself from the bricks and leapt up onto the bench, flickering through the sunlight and shade that danced across the pink paint.

'What is that?' Jessie gasped and drew up her feet.

'That's Blot.' Greenwood reached onto the bench and picked up a handful of black. 'Blot's the Timecatcher cat; met her when I was shut inside. She

51

followed me out; been with me ever since. She's all right, is Blot.'

The shadow nosed Greenwood's beard for a moment, then leapt gracefully back onto the bench. It was like watching water spill through the air; she seemed to ripple from grey to black and back again as she jumped. The movement was pure cat but Jessie could only briefly make out a flicker of paw, a swish of tail, a glance of ear, as Blot disappeared back into the shadows. On the ground Duff tensed briefly then relaxed as if to say, 'Nothing there, and I have bigger bones to bury.' He went back to watching Greenwood.

Jessie tore her gaze away from the benchtop where the darkness rippled rhythmically as the shadow cat washed her fur. 'Is Sully Ellz'mede still in there?'

'He came out last time Timecatcher were open. Came out cacklin' and whoopin' about the "Spark" and how, when he had the "Spark" in his possession, 'twould set him free.'

'Spark?'

'I think that's what he calls the source. He musta found the day 'tis hid in. I locked him in place for a while but I had to let him go eventually. Then he just laughed and shot off over the roof and was gone. Haven't seen sight nor shade o' him for past seven years. I hear he's in Dublin, in the city. But Sullivan Ellz'mede is obsessed with the Timecatcher; he'll be back any day now.' Greenwood looked over at the corner where the four steps ran up to the bricks. Nat and Jason and Jessie followed his gaze.

'The portal?' Jessie whispered to Jason.

'That's where it is, or will be in four days' time.'

'This is a seventh year?' Jessie's eyes popped. 'It's going to open? Next *week*?' She jumped to her feet and stared at the steps and the wall above them.

'Yes. That's why it's important this stays secret, Jessie. There was a door at the top of those steps when the mill was first built. A worker walked through it one summer's day and disappeared into thin air, never to be seen again. Unfortunately for him he had walked through the door just as the portal opened. Master Greenwood says the poor man dropped down through the vortex like a stone and probably died from the impact wherever he landed. People blocked up the doorway after that.'

'Oh!' Jessie said. 'So that's why you grabbed me yesterday.'

'Yes!' Jason smiled. 'It's up to me and Nat to keep the living safe from the Timecatcher. We'll make sure no one but ourselves comes into this room while the portal is open. We need to keep this place as people-free as possible over the next few days. It's important no one gets hurt. Master Greenwood will have to do his best with any ghost-traffic.'

'Just because folks nowadays don't know much o' magic or how to use it doesn't mean it can't hurt them,' Greenwood said gravely. 'And as long as the magic is there and there is a way to access it, someone will be tryin' to steal it.'

'Sullivan Ellz'mede,' said Jessie.

'Sully Ellz'mede,' said Greenwood.

'Master Greenwood has asked us to help him figure

out what's in there.' Nat turned to Jessie. 'It is our number-one case. Top priority.'

'Can I help? Please let me help. I'm good at history; I've got a good memory. I won't get in the way.' Please, please, she thought.

'I don't know.' Jason wrinkled his forehead. 'Master Greenwood?'

Greenwood rubbed his beard thoughtfully. 'I've tried to avoid askin' for help over the years but when Jason and Nat fetched up in these very rooms, at this very time, and they bein' people who deal in findin' out secrets – it seemed like fate was takin' a hand in things. You're here now, Jessie Minahan; did fate send thee, too? Well, we'll see whether you be a help or a hindrance. I'm more worried about thy friend.'

'My friend?' Jessie looked down at Duff in surprise.

'Not him – him!' Greenwood raised his huge hands towards the door of the back room and a look of intense concentration formed on his face. There was a sucking, swooshing sound and arms and legs came dragging through the door followed by the scowling face and wriggling body of a boy.

'Well, Master G. You've been listenin'. You knows it all now. Hindrance or help; which do you mean to be?'

✳✶ 9 ✳✶

A gull swooped low over the multiple roofs of the mill. It flew out over the street and once around the outside of the building then dipped back in towards the yard. Anyone watching it might have noticed an occasional jerking quality to the bird's flight, the kind of movement a mechanical toy plane makes when its operator is new to the controls. It thumped to a halt on the Button Factory roof and perched in the gutter. Its head went from side to side as it watched a girl and a dog walk across the yard and up the back stairway. It watched as the door opened and girl and dog went inside. The windows beneath the gutter were ajar and the gull seemed to be listening. For quite a long time. Then with a raucous 'garachh' it was off and gliding back towards the city's centre.

'Ah me, and wouldn't everyone fly if they could, my pretty?' said the voice inside the bird's head as it turned left at the river and followed the line of the water past one bridge and then another. 'Let's go higher, Pretty. Let's have some fun.'

The bird, intent on getting back to its flock, resisted for a moment but the voice-thing inside its head took control and jerked it upwards.

'I'm getting the hang of this now, Pretty, Pretty. I'm

finding my wings; it's not so flapping difficult, flap, flap. Oh, don't fret so, birdbrain, you'll get back to your friends soon enough. Up, up, my pretty. Ah, sure, I feel like a king, king of all Dublinia ... oh all right, spoilsport; you want to go down, let's go down.'

The voice let go its insidious grip and the gull, confused, was free-falling towards the water. It pulled itself out of the spin with the surface of the water only three beaks away. The Ha'penny Bridge was within sight now and the gull started determinedly towards it. For a few moments it was itself again, thinking only of food and its favourite perch on the top of a nearby high-rise. Then the world turned upside down, once, twice, three times; the gull could feel the unnatural strain of the movements searing through its feathers. The bridge was close, the approach way too fast. The bird screeched in terror as the voice flipped them sideways. They shot under the bridge, then out the other side and up and up, too high again. Down in a loop, and another and another. A sharp pain jab-jabbed just behind the bird's eyes.

On the Ha'penny Bridge the passing crowd stopped to stare at the gull's strange antics; people were pointing and laughing and taking photos with their mobile phones. Another series of spins and dives and it was all over. The gull seemed to jerk and fall, regain flight and skim drunkenly across the water. It landed on the Liffey boardwalk, wobbled, and sat down heavily on the wooden surface. A ripple of applause broke out across the bridge and people began to move away.

But this show had a second act. Herring gulls began

to circle, then land around the exhausted bird. Some sidled towards it and a few hovered ominously overhead, others watched from the river's walls. 'Pretty' shrank down and hunched its head between its wings. There was a moment when people and gulls were quiet, then the birds attacked. The triple-somersaulting gull disappeared in a halo of beaks, wings and claws. The crowd on the bridge let out a horrified gasp and turned away.

'Dear me, Pretty, what a grim lot your friends are. How sharp their beaks are, how deliciously sharp. Poor fishbreath. You should have stuck with me. My, my, how your feathers fly.'

Sullivan Ellz'mede tut-tutted and shook his head sorrowfully. He had a good view of the boardwalk from this lamppost. As a ghost he could hover, glide and drift, but hitching a ride in a gull had been a . . . blast. Blast? Was that this year's word or was that *so* last decade? Well, as long as it wasn't so last century. Yes, flying was a blast. Really flying, inside skin and bone, feeling heartbeats, inhaling air. Exhilarating. Life, any life, was better than this insipid perpetual floating.

His newfound talent for borrowing bodies was the business, the real deal. Over the last seven years he had spent part of nearly every day trying out some animal or other. He'd tried street cats and urban foxes, dogs, birds, insects. He had even been to the zoo. The tiger that had gone berserk and tried to jump its enclosure? That was Sully. Stupid thing wouldn't have hurt itself so if it had just given in and done what Sully wanted. A few spectacular growls and a bit of crowd scaring – had that really been too much to ask?

The smaller the animal the more control he could assert over its mind. They all fought him to some extent but the bigger the mammal the harder it was for Sully to stop it pushing him back out. He had tried primates of course – monkeys, apes – but he couldn't get a firm enough grip on their brains to stay even five minutes.

And people weren't possible.

Yet.

But the Timecatcher would open again soon. When he, Sully, had that magical thing he'd found inside it in his grasp, people would be possible at last. A body of his own again, a living, breathing body. He had the perfect one picked out already. But, for now, he'd have to make do with smaller, more manageable creatures.

Insects were simple but not much use. And so bloomin' fragile. Rats. Rats were best. Quick, quiet, agile. And easy to control. Sully could achieve a lot with a rat. Oh yes, life is a wonderful thing. Any life, any heartbeat. Sully surveyed the mess of feathers and bird bits below.

'Ah me, Pretty; Pretty is no more. See how jealous our old friends get when we are different, Pretty? See how ugly they turn? Get a notion to better yourself, try something new, and do your friends applaud, say well done, clever old you? Oh no, Pretty. Not them. All they want to do is tear you down.'

✴✴ 10 ✴✴

No more games, no more make-believe. A real adventure, with real people. And a dog. G had always wanted a dog.

'Yahoo!' His voice echoed around the empty yard.

He emerged fully into the sun and floated towards the mill gate. It wasn't open yet. He'd been awake ages now.

Footsteps, panting, out on the street. Jessie and Duff? He had to know. He stuck his head through the gate and, sure enough, girl and dog were standing outside. It was Saturday morning so there was no one else to be seen the length of Brunswick Street.

'What time is it?' G made himself visible, Jessie jumped, then turned her head away crossly.

'Seven thirty-two,' she snapped.

'Yer early, Jason said eight.'

'The sooner we get started the more we'll get done.'

'There's no one else here yet,' G said helpfully.

'I figured that out for myself, thank you.' Jessie leaned against the gate. Duff snuffled around at the base of the wall. 'I don't know why Master Greenwood has let you be part of this, anyway.'

'He probably figures it's safest to have me where he can keep an eye on me.' G wasn't eejit enough to think Greenwood had had a complete change of heart and now they were going to be the best of friends. Didn't matter, but. He had asked G to help and G had agreed, quick-fast, before Greenwood changed his mind.

'Well, I suppose Master Greenwood knows what he's doing.' She sniffed.

G pulled his head back into the yard.

Hmmm! She's still mad at me, he thought. I suppose I can't really blame her.

He frowned. He had hoped she'd be over the pushing stuff by now. He had apologised, hadn't he? But then, he had tried to turn her ghost.

Turn her ghost? spluttered a little voice deep inside him. *Don't you mean k—*

Shut up, you! mumbled G. It had seemed like such a good idea at the time.

Selfish, said the little voice. *Just plain bad.*

'Jessie?' G stuck his head back through the gate.

'What?' She pursed her lips.

''M sorry, okay? 'Bout yesterday. The pushing thing. I didn't mean it . . .'

She looked at him directly now. A slow, incredulous stare. G felt himself glow pink.

'Well, yes, I–I–I did mean it. But just for a second. Then I thought better of it and pulled you back in.'

'Wow! Thanks a bunch for not killing me. You're too kind.' Jessie said scornfully. 'To what do I owe the change of heart?'

'My gran.' G's voice was gruff.

'Your gran? Is she here too?' Jessie scanned the wall

as if she expected another spectre to pop through it from some odd angle.

'No. Gran's not dead,' G said with a snort. Then he paused. He'd never thought of that before. After all this time, maybe she was.

Dead.

Gran.

He blinked. Jessie watched him from behind that curtain of hair.

'She's not. She can't be.' G's forehead creased and the gash on his temple gaped clearly through his fringe. 'I can't remember anyone properly, just her. Gran can't be dead.' He glared at Jessie.

'Okay, okay.' Jessie shifted her weight against the gate. 'Can't you remember anything?'

'Nothing much. Bits. Lots of blanks. My gran. Not so much her face, more things she'd say. Telling me off, mostly. Putting me straight on stuff. And stories. She was great at telling stories, my gran. But she'd not have liked me making you fall yesterday, just so as I could have someone to talk to always. I thought that as soon as I done it. So I pulled you back in.'

'You pushed me out that door because you wanted to have someone to talk to always?' The girl's face softened and G turned pink again.

'Here's Jason's car,' he said quickly, looking away.

A battered white car with a number plate older then Jessie stopped on the road, indicator flashing. Jason waved from the driver's seat and Nat jumped out, jangling a set of keys.

'Good morning, you guys.' She was all in purple

today, beads on her skirt tinkled as she moved towards the gate. 'Are you ready for some hard work? And how is Duffy-Woofy today?'

Jessie helped push back the gates. G stayed inside his for the ride, popping out the front of it when it trundled into the wall. Duff ran after Nat as she crossed the yard and headed up the back stairs.

'Coffee,' said Jason, as he got out of the car. 'That's the first order of the day, methinks.'

'A good tankard o' ale is what I'm needin', if I could only drink it.' Greenwood was suddenly there, sweeping in above their heads. He landed beside Nat at the top of the steps and waited politely while she turned the key in the lock. By the time Jessie and Jason reached the door the others were inside. Duff was dancing around Nat's ankles like a puppy, buttons flying around the floor. G floated in and stationed himself in an empty corner.

Greenwood passed his huge hand over his face wearily.

'I've been in Dublin city all night tryin' to get any ghost I could find to talk to me. Askin' them for news o' Sullivan Ellz'mede.' He was fading in the sunlight; G had to squint to keep him in focus.

'Anything?' asked Jason anxiously.

'Yes,' said Greenwood flatly. 'And it's not good.'

✳✻ 11 ✳✻

'*D*on't know what was goin' on – seemed like every spectre in the city was avoidin' me. Strange ...' Greenwood frowned, almost disappeared then shook himself visible again. 'The one or two I did manage to corner insisted they knew nothin' o' Sully's whereabouts. Then I met ol' Jonathan. He was right pickled; he'd spent the day sleepin' in a vat o' Guinness down James's Gate.'

Jason drained his coffee. 'Get any sense out of him at all?'

'He was jabberin'. Nonsense, mostly. He kept sayin', "I'm not to tell, I'm not to tell", so I says, all a whisper, "What are you not to tell?" and he says, "Sully's in the old bottle factory down the docklands". So off I went.'

Greenwood rubbed his beard. 'The old bottle factory has been turned into a fancy office. Name on door read "Narls Cunningham". I had a look around. The computer was covered in those little sticky bits o' paper like you use.'

'Post-its?' suggested Nat, waving a pink one in the air.

The big ghost nodded. 'One had "NB sausages and woodchips for Ratty-boy" written on it.'

'A pet?' suggested Jason.

'A room-mate?' suggested Nat, and everyone laughed.

'Another bit o' paper had the word "TIMECATCHER" in big letters.'

All laughter stopped. Jessie looked at G in alarm. Jason swung his chair around to face the computer and flexed his fingers. He hit the 'on' button and the machine chimed into life. He indicated to Jessie to pull up her seat and beckoned G closer. 'NARLS CUNNINGHAM' he typed, and clicked the 'search' box.

'Okay. Let's see what we've got.' Jason rubbed his hands together. 'Newspaper article. "Narls Cunningham. One of the city's brightest independent television producers." Hmmm. Let's have a look at you, Mr Cunningham.' Click.

Jessie watched over Jason's shoulder as a face filled the screen. Mousy brown hair followed by watery, pale-blue eyes, a large nose, an insincere smile, a barely-there chin dotted with pimples, and the shoulders of an expensive suit two sizes too big.

'What d'ya think?' Jason hit 'print'.

'Smarmy,' Jessie decided, wrinkling her nose. 'Weird eyes.'

'Slimy.' G nodded.

'So, Sully has been telling this guy about the Timecatcher?' Jason caught the print as it rolled out. He swung back to face Greenwood. 'Any idea why?'

'Well, underneath "TIMECATCHER" were the words "historical reality TV" and "multi-channel".'

Greenwood pronounced the words slowly and carefully. 'What does it all mean?'

Nat pulled a face. 'It means this Narls person sees the Timecatcher as a big showbiz opportunity. He wants to exploit it for money. This is terribles.'

'It's kind of genius, actually.' Jason threw up his hands in despair. 'What an *amazing* idea. He gets into the Timecatcher, puts in a load of cameras, and he's got access to centuries – worth of "live" action.'

'My guess is 'tis some sort o' diversion,' said Greenwood. 'Sully is usin' that young man to get to the power source. I know Sully. Nothin' for nothin', that's him.'

'We can assume Sully's after the magical object that controls the Timecatcher.' Jason leaned back in his seat. 'He may know where it is but he can't move it without help, so he's sold the idea of the Timecatcher as a money-making machine to Cunningham in the hope Cunningham will work out a way to move it for him. Could that be it?'

'But—' Jessie chewed her lip and thought hard. 'Wouldn't the cameras get smashed up? How would they keep the Timecatcher open? How would the power source react to their presence? And I thought people couldn't survive in there?' She looked at the photo in her hand. The weird eyes looked back at her. Cold, blank eyes. Fish eyes in a creepy suit.

'Might it be possible for living people to travel in the Timecatcher lowering themselves down on ropes attached to something out here?' asked Jason, turning to Greenwood.

'Maybe.' Greenwood nodded.

'And once you travel through the vortex and reach the tree, is the actual ground beneath your feet solid?'

Greenwood nodded again. 'Everythin' else is shadow, but the earth is solid enough.'

'So, if Narls Cunningham figures out a way to get people in there he *might* be able to put in equipment and film,' suggested Jason. 'Once the cameras were in place transmitting from different days the portal could close and the pictures would just keep rolling. They'd have to find a way to power the cameras indefinitely, but it may be doable.'

'Hmm,' Nat mused. 'Narls runs his reality shows and, in return, Sully gets him to fetch the power source for him. Sully's swapping his knowledge of the Timecatcher, and the potential it has, for help getting the power source out.'

'But if Sully moves the source won't that – I dunno – collapse the 'catcher somehow?' asked G. He was concentrating so hard his eyebrows were meeting in the middle.

'Aye, it might, boy. But this Narls Cunningham don't know that, do he?' Greenwood had begun pacing. 'Once Sully gets what he wants he won't care what happens to his "friend" and his big ideas.'

'And if the 'catcher collapses,' persisted G. 'What then?'

'Maybe nothin'. Maybe that'd be the end o' the Timecatcher altogether.' But Greenwood didn't look like he believed that. An uneasy frown creased his brow. 'I'm afraid, like I said before, that the collapse o'

Timecatcher would somehow shatter time.'

Jessie caught her breath. Shatter time. The past infects the present. It couldn't actually happen, could it? Time changing. People disappearing as if they'd never been. People who had never been, being.

Suddenly the Timecatcher felt very real, something tremendously powerful and, at the same time, terribly fragile.

And somewhat less of a mystery-history project.

✳✳ 12 ✳✳

The back room was dark and shadowy. At the far end of the room, in front of a small window, a rack of assorted clothes stood beside a full-length mirror. A table beside the mirror was covered in make-up, jewellery, a bowl of false noses and what appeared to be a row of heads. Cardboard boxes littered the floor. One held bags – handbags, shopping bags, briefcases. Another was full of shoes and boots, another held assorted hats and helmets and another trailed hair of various shades over every edge.

But the chaos on the floor gave way to order on the walls. A heavy red line was drawn at eye level from one edge of the door right around the walls to the other side. Arrows, maps, photos, sheets of statistics and information were tacked neatly above and below the line. Everything was carefully labelled.

'Wow!' G was moving through the boxes on the floor. 'Look at all this stuff.'

'What's that?' asked Jessie, pointing to the wall.

'That's our timeline,' said Jason. 'We've gone back as far as 3000 BC. There's information on different cultures that have lived in this area; events, battles, individuals who've passed this way over the centuries. Anything that might help us figure out what the source of power inside the Timecatcher is.'

Jessie and G moved closer to have a look. At the start of the line there wasn't so much information, just some images of standing stones and dolmens and druids. Around the fifth century AD the walls started to get quite busy and by the ninth there was something for every single year of each century.

'Looks fascinating.' Jessie's eyes sparkled as she headed straight to the bit labelled 'Viking Dublin'.

'Looks boring,' G said under his breath; aloud, 'How did you choose where to start? Why "circa 3000 BC"?'

'That's the earliest the Timecatcher goes – a rough guess on Greenwood's part. And—' Jason held up his hand as G and Jessie both began to speak at once '—I know what you're thinking: surely the earliest day in there is the day that the Timecatcher came into being?'

G and Jessie looked at each other and nodded.

Jason shook his head. 'The power source seems to have generated shadow days backwards through time as well as forwards. It has cloaked itself in ancient days as well as new ones, so it could be anywhere.

'The oak tree only appears as a sapling around 2500 BC and disappears around AD 1506, which is far too old for any tree, so the power source must have magically extended its life. Then, in 1762, this mill was built where the oak once grew.' Jason picked up a button that had strayed in from the front room.

'Five thousand years' worth of days,' Jessie said eagerly.

'That's a lot of days.' G pulled a face.

Jason flipped the button in the air and caught it with

one hand. 'Right! But the last eight hundred years' worth can be discounted – we're only interested in the days before Master Greenwood accidentally created the portal. That still leaves four thousand two hundred years' worth to search. When Master Greenwood is in the Timecatcher he can only check out the days one at a time and he's only had three days every seven years in which to do it.'

'But he searched it for seven years, the time he got shut in,' said Jessie.

'He said when he was in there, the power source seemed to be playing tricks on him, messing with his memory. Any time he felt he was getting close to it he'd find himself getting confused. After a while he couldn't remember which days he'd searched and he suspects he may have visited the same days over and over.'

'You sure he isn't making it all up?' G snorted. 'I mean it all sounds a bit mad, doesn't it?'

Jessie raised an eyebrow. 'Well, last week I would have thought ghost boys flying in and out of walls was a pretty crazy idea.'

Jason smiled.

'Greenwood's been dead a long time, but.' G shrugged. 'He could be completely barmy. I've been here ages and I've never seen the Timecatcher. Or Sullivan Ellz'mede neither.'

Jason pursed his lips. 'Greenwood figures you're dead at least ten years. Sully Ellz'mede hasn't been near the mill for the last seven years and the previous seven he was inside the Timecatcher, so, logically, you'd never have seen him.'

G pulled a face.

'There's something I don't understand,' said Jessie. 'Master Greenwood can go through walls, so why can't he just go in there now – why does he need the portal to open?'

'Apparently that's the one wall he can't pass through, Jessie,' Jason said. 'Master Greenwood said he's tried it from every angle. Seems the only way into the Timecatcher, even for ghosts, is through the portal.'

Jessie pointed to a large label marked 21st June 1201. 'That's the day Greenwood opened it.'

'Yep. After that we've tacked on a few significant dates – Greenwood's hanging in July and the year the mill was built – but that pretty much ends the timeline.' Jason waved his hands at the walls. 'We've looked at all this *so* many times we can't see the wood for the trees. That's where you guys come in. Throw your eyes and brains over this lot, make a note of anything, and I mean *anything*, that jumps out at you and – what on earth is Duff doing?'

Duff had been sniffing around ever since they entered the room. Now he was snuffling noisily around the box of wigs. Having given it a good going over with his nose, he jumped in and turned once, twice, three times. With a happy sigh, he lay down, grey fur against a pile of red, brown, black and blonde.

'No, Duff!' Jessie made to grab his collar but Jason just laughed.

'Those are all fairly well banjaxed already. I didn't realise wigs needed to be stored carefully until Nat came along and insisted we get these stands for them.' He indicated the row of heads on the table. 'She managed to rescue a few and that box got the rejects. Duff has found a good use for them.'

Jessie grinned. 'Okay!' She pulled a small notebook and pen out of her jeans pocket. 'There's a ring mentioned here, with the Viking stuff. The Ring of—' she checked a label on the wall '—Tomar.'

'Yeah, I had high hopes for that one. It was stolen – when does it say?'

'AD 994.'

'Right. But no amount of searching the web got me any information on who, what or where Tomar was. So we figure it was just the possession of some minor Viking family or something. It went from a code red label to a yellow one fairly quickly.' Jason indicated the labels that were dotted around the walls. 'Yellow means "worth a bit more research", orange means "possibly significant", and red means "top priority".'

'There aren't many reds,' G remarked. He stifled a yawn.

'No. There were to begin with, but we've been working our way through and downgrading as we go. But don't let that influence you – like I said, we need fresh thoughts on all this.' Jason gazed at the walls for a moment as if something new might jump out at him if he stood there long enough. 'Right!' He turned back to Jessie and G. 'I'll leave you to it. I need to get my head around how to stop Sully and this Cunningham chap.' And he went out to the front room where Nat was working on her computer, and closed the door.

Jessie gave a sigh just as contented as Duff's. She had covered some of this already in history class – the very early bits and some of the recent stuff. This was going to be fun.

'Hey, Coaly-Cat.' G waved as a black shadow sloped through a wall and flickered along the bricks.

Jessie glanced up. 'That's Blot. At least that's what Greenwood said.'

'Oh? I've always called him Coaly-Cat. We're mates, Coaly-Cat and me. He sometimes comes and hangs out. We just sit quiet-like for an hour or so.'

'She,' Jessie said absently over her shoulder.

'What?'

'She. Coaly-Cat – I mean, Blot – is a she.'

'Says who?'

'Says Greenwood.'

'What would he know?' G looked at the cat with a frown.

'She's his cat. She's the Timecatcher cat. Greenwood found her in there and brought her out, ages ago.'

'Oh.'

'I thought you were listening in on us yesterday evening?'

'Couldn't hear everything, could I?' G said, rather sharply. He examined the rack of clothes. It was filled from end to end, one half with women's things, the other half with men's. Blot strolled through his feet. G ignored her.

'Bet that blonde wig would look mad on,' G suggested, surveying the cardboard box Duff had settled in.

'I'm busy.' Jessie was back at the bit of timeline labelled 'Viking'.

'Is that a pink one?' G leaned down to the box, almost nose to nose with Duff.

'A pink wig?' Jessie laughed. 'No one has pink hair.'

'I can't tell; Duff is on it.'

'Oh, for heaven's sake.' Jessie put down her notebook and pen and went over to the wig box. Sure enough a strand of violently pink hair was just visible under Duff's right ear; she gave it a tug. The dog blinked.

'Sorry, Duffer.' Jessie lifted Duff's head and pulled out a pink mess of curls.

'Put it on,' begged G. 'Go on.'

Jessie laughed and brought the wig over to the mirror. She leaned her head down, pulled the wig on like a swimming cap and straightened up.

G snorted and Jessie burst out laughing. 'What on earth do they use this for? It's nuts!'

'Try those on—' G pointed to a set of yellow overalls '—and these—' a pair of 1950s horn-rimmed glasses '—and those—' hob-nailed boots.

A few minutes later the results had them howling. Duff watched, his head cocked first to one side, then the other. Blot sprang up onto a shelf to get a better view.

'What's going on?' Jason burst through the door. Jessie hastily pulled off the wig and glasses and tried to look serious but G guffawed and she started to giggle too.

'Look—' Jason sounded annoyed '—today is the 17th of June. The Timecatcher opens in three days and the

74

source will be at its strongest the very next day. This may seem like a game to you but it's actually very, very serious. And we haven't got time for you two to be larking around in here, making a mess.'

Jessie turned red and kicked off the boots. G bit his lip and snickered slightly. Just once.

'Right!' Jason snapped. 'Either you are in or out. It's work and focus, or there's no place for you here.'

G bent his head and bit his lip twice as hard. He peeked out from under his fringe and tried to catch Jessie's eye but she was busy shedding the yellow overalls. Above their heads Blot leapt from her perch and drifted gracefully to the floor, passing straight through Jessie as she went.

'That was weird.' Jessie blinked and laughed. 'And it tickled.'

Jason glowered.

G saw an odd look cross Jessie's face.

'Books!' She shook her head slightly, as if shaking away a daydream. 'I've got to look at books.'

She kicked the overalls away and headed to the door, picking up her notebook as she left.

✳✳ 13 ✳✳

G walked around the walls twice, running his fingers along the timeline as he went. Like looking into a bush. And about as much fun, now he was on his own. He stopped at AD 1201 and read the transcript of Greenwood's account of accidentally opening the portal, and how he'd let himself get caught rather than expose the Timecatcher.

I'd have got all those soldiers up that tree and pushed them in, one after the other, G thought. Then I'd have scarpered, quick-fast. He must be mad, letting them take him when he knew they'd hang him.

There was the label marking Greenwood's death: 5th July 1201.

If G could just write stuff down maybe he could make something out of all these words; it was too much to try holding it all in his head at once.

I can't do anything, he thought crossly. Can't do computer stuff, can't leave the building to find out stuff, can't work out stuff in a stupid notebook. Not without Jessie's help, anyway. 'S no good now she's gone.

Just when she seemed to have forgiven him for the pushing thing, too.

'Time for a change of scene,' he announced to Blot, who was back up on the shelf, watching him. 'If Jessie just took off, so can I. And I don't need any kitty-cat company, either.'

A tour of the artists' studios would have to do. He hadn't been around them for at least a week now. He floated across to the other side of the building. Lunchtime. No one in yet. He'd start in Studio One and work his way back towards the Button Factory.

The woman in Studio One was into painting tiny people in tiny coffins at the moment. Cool! B plus. The guy in Studio Two painted flowers, giant blooms in pink and green. Not cool. Double E.

Studio Three was his favourite. The woman was quite old but she did abstract stuff in great colours. And big, she painted really big. Sometimes G would come here near dawn to wind down after a bad night. Just sit and stare. Her new piece was right up to scratch – A plus.

Studio Four was the nervous skinny guy's. He had a tic in his left eye that G liked to twitch. It only took one tube of paint to hit the floor, or 'rubbish' rasped in his ear to set him off.

His paintings *are* rubbish anyway, G thought, wrinkling his nose at the new canvas. This month's painting – they took him forever – was of a man drinking coffee under a cloud upon which sat a howling dog. Was it supposed to be clever or what? Pah! C for technique, E for content. Must try harder.

It wasn't fair. G was certain-sure he'd been good at art when he was alive. He knew he could paint better than Nervous Skinny. Maybe even as good as the woman in Studio Three. He'd been watching them all paint for years now, maybe ten years, according to Jason.

That's forever, he thought. Like going to art college. I'd be a professor by now if I was alive. Professor G! Ha ha.

But all the stuff he'd learnt from watching meant nothing if he couldn't actually lift a brush. And he couldn't. Never since that one time, long ago.

He was drifting into Studio Five when he heard noises coming from Six.

'That one's been empty for ages,' he remarked to the adjoining wall. 'Okay! Let's see what we've got!' He passed through.

A tall man was standing in the centre of the room considering a blank canvas perched on an easel. Hmm. None of the other artists used easels, they just taped canvas straight onto the wall.

The man went still for a moment and turned around slowly. He was staring at the exact spot where G was floating.

Uh, oh. G looked down at his body, but he was still in invisible mode.

What's he gawking at? G wondered. He can't see me, can he?

The man was frowning now and he started to move uncertainly across the floor towards G. G floated away quickly and settled by the window. The guy stopped and turned his head; his eyes seeming to follow G. G whisked over him to the door. The guy continued staring at the window, then shook his head and turned back to the canvas.

That was freaky, G thought, puffing up his cheeks and mimicking a sigh of relief. Did I say something out loud? Did he sense me? Nah. Nah, he can't have.

The man was dressed all in black – black policeman shoes, black jeans, black T-shirt, black hair neatly trimmed except for a fringe falling across his forehead. G stared for a moment. There was something about the man's eyes. Something familiar? G searched his brain, trying to separate blurs from blanks. Nah, nothing.

The guy had obviously just moved in; the room was ridiculously tidy for an artist's studio. Empty canvases were stacked in ascending size by the wall and on a table beside the easel, paints were arranged in two rows of tubes, starting with white and moving through the colours like a chart – yellow, orange, red on through to black. G could see he was an amateur.

Way too many shades, mate, he thought. Let's see: five different yellows, six blues, two blacks. Wow! Never heard of mixing? And you've never used any of those before, have you? He eyed the jars of pristine brushes.

I could teach this guy a thing or two. G yawned. Okay, Painterman. When you gonna paint? The guy hadn't moved now for a full ten minutes. G was getting seriously bored. Ah yes! At last. Here we go! What colour is gonna hit that canvas first?

But Painterman walked away from the canvas to a CD player in the corner. He flicked it on.

Ramones. Cool choice, Painterman. Hey ho, let's go! G hit the air guitar. Now paint!

But the man just stood there, staring at the canvas.

I could always give him a nudge, G considered. Toss

the Burnt Sienna in his direction – hint, hint? Maybe sing along to a few bars of 'Judy is a Punk'. That'd get him moving.

You shouldn't be mean, whispered that annoying little voice, deep inside.

Who asked you? thought G.

But he'd keep the rules all the same; he didn't want to find himself banned from the detectives' rooms again, not now there was stuff happening. Real stuff. Jessie might come back. She would come back. Wouldn't she?

He drifted through the wall to the corridor and looked out into the yard. Ten years since his accident. Maybe more, Jason said. Maybe he'd been dead as long as he'd been alive. He was twelve when he died, he remembered that all right.

I don't suppose birthdays since then count, he thought. I'm still twelve. How come I can remember my age but not my name? And my gran, but no one else? He'd never given it much thought before.

I remember everything since I turned ghost, though. Most days here are the same as the next but I haven't forgotten them. I remember every painting every artist has painted. I remember every time Coaly-Cat came by for a visit. And every time Greenwood bothered to speak to me.

He could feel something like a ghost-tear forming in his eye. He blinked furiously.

Movement in the yard below caught his eye. A dog galloped across to the back stairs, wagging his stumpy tail.

'Jessie 'n' Duff are back,' G whispered to the wall. He felt a silly grin spread across his face as he somersaulted through the bricks into the Button Factory rooms.

✳✳ 14 ✳✳

$\mathcal{J}$essie ran up the steps two at a time, her notebook clutched tightly in her hand. She took a deep breath and hesitated at the open door. Jason was busy at his computer and seemed in better humour. Nat was at the printer, tugging out jammed paper. Master Greenwood was in a corner, shaking himself awake.

Jason glanced up from his screen. 'So, you're back then, young Jess?'

'Yeah.' Jessie cleared her throat. 'I've found something, I think.'

'Aha!' Jason eyed the notebook in Jessie's hand. 'Where did you hare off to earlier?'

'The library.' She flipped her notebook open. 'My dad used to say that the Internet was a great source of information but you should double-check it with a book.'

'The computer is magic, but!' G's eyes gleamed. 'It's like having your own library stuffed inside a little box.'

'Well, yeah. But anyone can post information on the Internet, right?' Jessie looked at Jason uncertainly. 'And you said you couldn't find much on the ring so I decided to go check out the library.'

'And?'

'I found an old book on Vikings in the history section; I took notes.' She turned a few notebook pages. 'The Ring of Tomar was a Viking ceremonial ring and it was stolen in AD 994 and never recovered.'

'We know that already,' said Jason impatiently. 'You've found something new. What?'

'Well, it said that the ring was stolen for an Irish chieftain who was a sworn enemy of the Vikings. He targeted the ring because it was really important to them. Apparently it was worn by all the Viking kings of Dublin and people would have sworn oaths on it and stuff.' Jessie looked up. Everyone was staring at her. Don't turn red, don't turn red. 'And in another book it said the ring was a sacred object, to do with Viking religion . . .' She tailed off.

'Thor.' Greenwood frowned. 'The Vikings worshipped Thor.'

'Did either book say anything about who or what Tomar was?' Jason had folded his arms and was rubbing his chin with one hand.

'Mmm, yes.' Jessie turned a page. 'Tomar was an ancestor of the Viking kings, they were known as the People of Tomar.'

'Could this be it?' Jason asked Greenwood. 'Could this be the power source?'

'Aye, it could. I was expectin' somethin' more ancient, somethin' further back than AD 994, but then the ring itself may be very old. May stretch back to Thor himself.'

Nat raised an eyebrow. '994 seems pretty long ago to me. Anything else, Jessie?' she asked. 'What did the Vikings do when their ring it was stolen?'

'They launched counter-raids but the Ring of Tomar was never seen again. Oh—' she flipped over another page '—and the librarian suggested I look up something called the *Annals of the Four Masters*, it's a really old history book. It dated the theft of the ring as M994.9, which I think means September in the year 994.'

'Oh, now you're just showing off!' Jason threw his arms up in mock despair. 'But you've earned the right; you've done brilliantly, Jessie.' He stood up. 'We'd better check something.' He led the way through to the back room.

'What are we looking for?' G sounded sulky.

Jessie glanced around at him and was rewarded with a glare. What's up with him now? she thought. He was never jealous? She shrugged and turned back to the timeline. Jason was peering at the dates after the theft of the ring.

'What is it?' asked Nat.

'The Vikings ruled Dublin and parts of Ireland, England and Wales, for several centuries. But, from what I can see here, after the theft of the Ring of Tomar they're really struggling to keep their grip on the city and all their strongholds. I think we might need a red Post-it; the ring is definitely a strong possibility for the power source.' He straightened up and turned to Jessie. 'Well done. We nearly missed this through my incompetence. I should have been more thorough; I gave up on the Ring of Tomar too easily. Good catch.'

'Okay,' said Nat. 'We may have figured out what the

source of power in the Timecatcher is, but what can we do about it?'

'That'll be up to G,' Greenwood said.

Jessie felt her mouth drop open in surprise, but she clamped it firmly shut. Nat's eyebrows nearly hit her hairline and an expression of complete confusion spread across Jason's face. They all turned to look at the boy. He was floating at a distance with his head down and his hands dug into his pockets.

'What?' he snapped: 'What are you all looking at?'

Greenwood glared at the sullen boy and gritted his teeth. 'We'll need thy help now, Pooka-boy. Whether you are up to the task or not is another thing altogether, but you're the only one of us can do what needs doin'.'

** 15 **

'*Y*ou have a skill. You can do somethin' only a few ghosts can do.' Greenwood's face was stern and he watched the boy closely. 'You can move things, after a fashion.'

G shifted his position slightly and peered up at Greenwood from under his fringe. 'So?'

'You'll need trainin' up; you'll need to work hard. You've much to learn and only a few days to learn it.'

'Learn what?'

G still sounded stroppy but there was such an expression of raw eagerness on his face that Jessie almost laughed. So that was what was bugging him; he was feeling left out. Eejit!

Greenwood shook his head at G's slowness. 'Learn to control that skill of thine, that's what. Instead o' just kickin' and shovin' things you need to learn to lift, hold, carry. You did it once before, when you lifted that paintbrush. You need to figure out how you did it so you can move things that need movin'.'

'What things?' G's eyes were huge. 'You mean – the ring?'

'O' course I mean the ring, what else would I mean?' Greenwood practically bellowed.

G flinched and his mouth formed a stubborn line. Jason coughed.

'Em, okay. So if G can move the ring, Master Greenwood—' Jason threw his hands up in a gesture of confusion '—well, *I'm* not really sure where you're going with this, either, actually ...' He tailed off as Greenwood sighed heavily.

'Look. Sully Ellz'mede must have some idea o' whereabouts o' the Ring o' Tomar. Why else is he makin' daft plans with this Cunningham man? He musta found it when he was trapped in the Timecatcher. He's been schemin' to make it his. We need to get to that ring first. Move it and hide it someplace he can't find it. That has to be our priority now – protectin' the source from Sully and his friend.'

'Ah, right, I see.' Jason still seemed puzzled. 'But if G carries the ring out of the Timecatcher won't that be just as likely to disturb time as Sully doing the same?'

'No one's takin' the ring out o' the Timecatcher.' Greenwood shook his head in exasperation. 'Me and the boy go in and find the ring before Sully does. Sully can't move it his self so he'll be needin' help from this Cunningham man. They must have a plan o' how to do it but, as you said before, they'll need to put in ropes and contraptions o' some sort.'

'To do that they'd have to have access to this room,' said Jason. 'And we're not going to make that easy for them.'

Greenwood nodded. 'So that gives us time. Now we know what month the ring is hidden in, we know which days to search – we find it before they get to it, then we hide it.'

'Where?'

'We hide it in another day – there are thousands. We keep the ring safe for the three days the portal is open, then put it back in its rightful place just before portal closes, then get out o' there.' Greenwood's face was grim. ''Twill have to work, I don't know o' any other way, dost thou?'

Jason leaned back in his chair and shook his head. 'So, young G, it all depends on you learning to control and fine-tune that power of yours.' The detective sounded doubtful.

Jessie could see G's face from where she sat. He looked as doubtful as Jason. Oh, come on, G, she entreated silently. You can do this.

She was sure he could; he had pulled her back into the building when he needed to.

'I taught many lads to use the longbow when I was alive,' Greenwood said. 'That's all about movement and control, the same sort o' skills the boy needs to learn if his talent for movin' things is to be o' any use. I'll try to instruct him, though 'twill probably send me screamin' to the banshees.'

Uh-oh, now G just looked fierce. Another minute and he'd be gone, disappearing through a wall. Think, think.

'Em . . .' they all turned to look at her.

'The kick-boxing club.'

'Yes?' Jason raised his eyebrows.

'Well, it opens tomorrow—'

'And?'

'They're running a free open day.' She deliberately avoided G's gaze. 'It will be full of local kids learning to do kick-boxing and tae kwon do. Tae kwon do's all about movement and control and stuff, right?'

'Brilliant!' Jason slapped his fist on the counter. The buttons bounced. 'That's it! G will have the best of tuition. Master Greenwood will teach him all he knows *and* G can observe the tae kwon do Master's class too. Excellent.'

Jason turned the computer screen towards Greenwood. 'Here, we'll look up a few tae kwon do sites and you'll see how useful it will be for G to study it. It's all about discipline and focus.'

'And I'm going to type up our new findings,' Nat said. 'So I will need your notes, Jessie, please.' Jessie handed them over and looked around for G. He had retreated to a corner, half-smiling, half-frowning.

'Think you can do it?' Jessie asked tentatively, moving over towards him.

'Why? You think I can't?'

'I think you can. So long as—'

'What? So long as what?'

'Well, you fly off the handle so easily and Greenwood, he's probably going to be pushing you hard. You can't just go running off when it gets tough.'

G glared.

Jessie tried again. 'Greenwood can be a bit gruff, you'll need to be patient and focus on learning.'

The boy made a noise that could have been annoyance or reluctant agreement. Wait. Say nothing. His eyes were hidden from her in the shadow of his fringe, his mouth pressed into an obstinate line again. Then suddenly he was smiling.

'I'm going to get into the 'catcher! Deadly! Wow! I didn't think Greenwood would let me go in there at all, now he'll be bringing me in himself. I'll surf it with him. Cool!'

'Surf it?'

'Yeah. The way he described catching the edge of a day and riding it in to the centre – it sounds like surfing, don't you think?'

Jessie nodded. 'It'll be amazing. You'll see all sorts of stuff; you have to promise to tell me all the details. Is there a day you want to see, one from history? One from your past?' Then she caught her breath. G was dead after all. There were days he wouldn't want to see again. There were days she wouldn't want to see again. Even the best ones might be sad. But G was so excited he didn't notice her concern.

'Oh, there'll be no time for that, we'll have work to do, me and Master Greenwood.' G took a deep breath, pulled back his shoulders and straightened himself. His eyes were shining. He thumped his fist down on the counter just as Jason had done. A small shower of buttons hit the floor.

'Yes!' he said. 'I can do it. I have two days to learn. I can move stuff; how hard can it be to lift stuff? Master Greenwood will teach me and I'll be like his apprentice. And I'll be patient—' he pulled a face at Jessie and she laughed '—me and Master Greenwood, we'll find the ring and keep it away from what's-his-face. It's going to be really cool. An adventure.'

'Right, lad.' Greenwood's voice booming across the room made them both jump. 'Time for our first lesson, let's get on with it.' He disappeared through the back-room door.

For a moment Jessie thought G wasn't going to follow him. He opened and shut his mouth a few times, turning a shade paler than usual. He took another deep breath, drew his shoulders back and drifted towards the back room.

'Good luck,' Jessie said.

'Thanks,' he croaked. He turned back to her. 'Jessie?'

'Yeah?'

'You done good today. The detective work in the library, I mean. Finding all that stuff in those boring old books. Cool. Well, not cool, really, but fair play to you anyway.'

'Thanks. I think.' She smiled at him and he grinned back.

Suddenly Greenwood stuck his head back through the wall. 'What are you standin' there for, boy? We don't have all night.' And he was gone again.

G stuck his tongue out at the bricks. 'Wish me luck,' he said to Jessie. 'I'll count to ten when things get bad, I promise!' He grinned and vanished.

Nat looked up from her computer. 'I have been checking out Viking ceremonial rings. It seems there's one on display in the National Museum.'

'Photo? Description?' asked Jason.

Nat scrolled down the screen. 'Nope. Neither.'

'We'll go and see it then—' Jason checked his watch

'—but it's too late now, they'll be closed. Tomorrow after lunch?' he asked.

Nat nodded.

'You too, Jessie?' Jason smiled at her. 'The ring is your breakthrough, after all. Want to come along and see if we can find out what's so special about these Viking rings?'

Jessie grinned. 'Absolutely!'

'Two pm at the museum, so,' Jason said. 'Is that thunder?' He went to the window. The sky had suddenly clouded over. The air was heavy and still.

The rain came just as Jessie reached Sitric Street. There was a deep rumble, a bright flash, and suddenly rain was drumming on the road, soaking her to the skin before she got to her front door.

✳✳ 16 ✳✳

It rained all night. On Sunday afternoon, as they left the museum, the sun came back out and the drenched streets and roofs glistened. Duff was waiting impatiently at the museum gate, looking damp and disgruntled. When Jessie untied him he shook himself thoroughly, getting everyone wet, then trotted along at their heels rather more cheerfully. More cheerfully than Jessie, Nat or Jason anyway.

'Back to the mill, then,' Jason said gloomily.

They walked on, crossing the Millennium Bridge and turning for Brunswick Street. Jessie fell behind. She had rainwater in her sandals; they squelched and her feet slid about inside them as she walked. She thought of G's face yesterday. Of how excited he had been. Telling G wasn't going to be easy.

Jason opened the door of the Button Factory so quietly G didn't even look up. Greenwood glanced around and mouthed 'shhh', indicating with his hand that they should stand still and watch.

G was staring intently at one single button on the counter top. It was a blue button, fairly large. His index finger was poised against it, shaking slightly. His tongue was caught between his teeth and his forehead was drawn down in a sharp crease between his eyebrows.

Greenwood was floating at a slight distance, watching. G took a breath and closed his mouth firmly. His eyes glazed over and his forehead relaxed. His finger was steady now and he moved it gently. The button began to travel across the counter, inch by inch, slowly, slowly, all the way to the edge. He stopped pushing and the button teetered, then dropped to the floor to join a particularly large heap of its mates.

G turned and saw Jessie and the others standing in the doorway. 'Did you see? I done it! I done it! I controlled the movement. I pushed that button real slow – no sudden movements, no kicking or shoving. Did you see?'

'Yes, we saw. Well done, G.' Jason summoned up one of his well-meaning smiles.

'Yez. That was brilliant, G,' Nat said.

Jessie nodded. She didn't say anything. Couldn't.

G didn't notice; he was completely high.

'The tae kwon do was deadly.' He turned back to the counter and began to push another button across the surface, this time snaking it this way and that. 'There were hundreds of kids. Most of them were useless, but a few of them copped on straight off the mark – those are the ones we watched. The instructor was a bit of a nerd but he knew his stuff. Like, you know, he was a pretty good teacher.'

The second button fell off the table and G made to catch it in his hand but it passed clean through.

'Rats! The teacher, he kept saying "don't let your

head get in the way". That means you have to think with your arm or your foot. That's where you send all your power, all your focus. It was really deadly.'

Greenwood almost smiled. 'Tomorrow we'll try liftin',' he said.

G drew his right hand back to his shoulder then shot his arm forward, hitting the back of one of the office chairs so that it went into a spin. He repeated the movement, slowly this time, and the chair came to a gentle stop at his hand. He looked up for applause, his eyes gleaming.

He laughed, then caught the glum expressions on their faces.

'What's wrong with you lot? You look like a funeral.'

Greenwood was staring at them too. 'What?' he asked sharply. 'What's wrong?'

Jason sighed. 'We've done some research and it seems the Ring of Tomar isn't a finger-ring. It's most likely a large, heavy ring intended to be worn around the neck. We've just seen a similar one in the museum and *I'd* find it a bit of a weight to carry.'

'This is the one we saw.' Nat flicked on the photo she had sneakily taken with her mobile phone and held it up. Against a black velvet backdrop, lit by three small spotlights, lay a huge ring. Three thick rods of silver twisted around each other to form a circle with a loop at one end and a catch at the other.

Jason glanced from Greenwood to the boy and made a sympathetic face. 'I'm sorry, G. This ring is an enormous thing and the Ring of Tomar is likely to be made of gold, so it will be even heavier. It weighs as much as a sack of flour; even if you could lift it, you wouldn't get it very far.'

Greenwood groaned. 'Now what'll we do? Hidin' it seemed the best way. The portal opens day after tomorrow. We need to come up with another plan; this has all been a big waste o' time.' He scratched his beard and wafted through the wall into the back room. Jason and Nat gathered up notebooks, pens and laptop and went there via the door.

Jessie looked at G. She saw the disappointment on his face. She saw it turn to disbelief. With one stroke he swept the counter and a hundred buttons flew in all directions, hitting walls and ceiling. One ricocheted off the computer and caught Duff on the side of the nose, making him yelp. Then G was gone.

A sound of crashing and smashing came dimly through the wall from the direction of the studios. Something glass, followed by the clatter of small things hitting cement. Then a heavy thud, as if something large and solid had made contact with the floor.

When Jessie reached the corridor on the other side of the building she realised the noise was coming from the end studio, the one that backed onto the Button Factory rooms. She ran to it and tried the door handle but it was locked.

'G!' She thumped on the door. 'Stop it, G! This isn't going to help. There'll be—'

'Something else for me to do? Oh, yeah? Like what?' Another crash.

'Like ... I don't know yet, but there will be. Please stop. Greenwood will be furious and then he'll banish you from the detectives' rooms again.'

'I don't care about him,' G yelled. Something else hit a wall. 'He's a fake, a fool. What kind of an eejit spends centuries worrying about some stupid hole in the air, anyway? Who cares if people find it? He's already dead, what's it to him? He just likes being in charge, bossing people around, acting as if he has to save the world. I hate him.'

He had stopped knocking things about. Jessie judged that he was just on the other side of the door. 'And Jason's as bad,' he snarled. 'All talk, no action. They're a bunch of wasters, playing at being heroes with their silly little quest.'

'It's not silly, G. It's really important. We're running out of time and if Sully steals the power source something awful could happen. What if the Timecatcher shatters? What if it changes history? Messes everyone up? Don't you care?' Jessie had both hands against the door and was talking straight to it as if she could see the boy hovering on the other side. 'Please, G. I know you're angry but you can't go wrecking some poor painter's stuff, even if you do think his work is no good. It's mean.'

There was a sniff from the other side.

'Anyway, you hurt Duff and you should apologise.' Jessie was pretty sure the worst was over now. If she could just get him out through the door to talk to her, everything would be okay. 'G?'

'Sorry, Duffer,' came a muffled voice too close to the

door and a hand came through the wood to stroke the dog's head.

That was just too much for Duff. He bit, his teeth going clean through the hand with a resounding snap. Jessie drew breath sharply and waited. The hand withdrew slowly and there was silence again.

'G?'

No answer.

'G?'

Nothing.

'G?'

'Who are you talking to?'

Jessie swung around. A tall man about the same age as Jason was standing behind her with a key in one hand and a bag with the name of an art shop in the other.

'This your dog? Hey there, fella. Aren't you a grand wee mutt, eh?' He put his keys into his other hand and leaned down to pat Duff and, to Jessie's relief, the little dog wagged his tail.

'So, who were you talking to just now?' The man looked up at Jessie curiously.

'A ghost.' Well, there was no point in beating around the bush. It was either tell the truth or say she had a habit of talking to doors. 'I'm sorry about your studio.' Jessie moved out of the way so the man could reach the lock.

'What do you mean?' He turned the key and pushed the door open. 'Phew! What a mess!' Jessie peered around his arm. It was worse than she'd expected. Paint was dribbling down the walls, canvases were torn and broken, splinters of wood and shards of glass covered the floor. CD cases were split open and the discs were lying in puddles of colour. An easel lay on its side and a table had landed on top of it. The painter was taking it quite well, really. Jessie would have expected anger, disbelief, maybe even a few accusations pointed in her direction – even though the door had been locked. 'A ghost did this? My name is George, by the way, George McCabe.'

'I'm Jessie,' said Jessie. 'And this is Duff.'

'There really is a ghost then?' George rolled up his sleeves and moved into the room, stepping carefully to avoid paint and glass. 'The other artists swore there was. I thought they were just having me on. They didn't say it was a poltergeist, but.'

'He's not. That is—' Jessie faltered '—he was upset about something. Do you want help cleaning up? I could give you a hand.'

'That'd be great, just mind the glass.'

'Okay.'

It took an hour. The painter seemed nice enough though Jessie thought it a bit odd that he didn't quiz her about G. He didn't seem very shocked by the idea of a ghost in his studio. He didn't ask her anything, not who the ghost was, how she knew him, what he was like, nothing at all. In fact he didn't have an awful lot to say for himself, did George McCabe. Not that Jessie was in the mood for talking. She needed to think.

By the time they finished cleaning up, it was evening.

'Do you think he'll just mess it all up again? This ghost boy?' asked the man. 'Have we been wasting our time?'

'I don't know,' Jessie said. 'I don't think so.'

Her head was buzzing. What if G was right? All talk, no action, he'd said. And it was true, they hadn't actually done anything about the Timecatcher but talk and talk and plan. And now those plans lay in shreds. They'd narrowly avoided making a huge mistake about the ring. She wondered if they'd missed something else, something important. Another mistake might mean they wouldn't stop Sully raiding the Timecatcher, and then what?

A bunch of wasters, playing at being heroes, G had called them. Jessie shivered. Suddenly it felt like everything was going wrong.

✳✳ 17 ✳✳

Later, when the mill was empty, Greenwood summoned G with a bellow.

'I mighta known,' the big ghost thundered as G skulked in the strange shadow shapes thrown by the Button Factory machines. 'You're nothin' but trouble. I was a fool to think any different, to think you had it in thee to do aught worthwhile. You think o' nothin' but thyself; you don't care an apple nor pear what we're tryin' to do here.'

He was pacing through the buttons, his anger making him glow an icy blue. G could see Blot flicker through the last pink rays of sun as they shrank back towards the sills of the Button Factory windows.

'Hast thou nothin' to say for thyself?' Greenwood snapped, glimmering angrily, inches from G's face.

G twisted that face into a scowl and opened his mouth, wanting to yell and shout at his old enemy, but no words came. To his own surprise, under Greenwood's gaze, he felt his head droop and found himself examining the floorboards through his feet. *Guilty as charged*, said the little voice inside. He retreated halfway through the wall.

'Ach!' Greenwood turned away from him in disgust. 'Get out o' my sight, Pooka-boy.'

G dropped through the floor into the gloom of the empty kick-boxing studio. The punch bag hung black, solid and huge in the grey light. He floated towards it. He squidged his eyes together and imagined it a head and limbs.

'Gotcha now, Master Greenwood!' he snarled. 'Take that. And that.'

Bam.

Bam, bam, bam.

Bam, bam, bam, bam.

He got into a rhythm. He could feel the bag swaying slightly in response to every punch. He could hear the contact he was making. Bam, bam, bam. It was dark now so he switched on his ghost light.

In the early days of being a dead thing floating around alone he had found it comforting to light the darkness of the old mill. Learning to control his inner light switch had taken ages. When he had finally got the hang of it, back in that first year, he had been so overjoyed he had giddily flicked himself on and off for hours. Like a drunk he hadn't been able to stop, and had spent the rest of the night miserably snapping on and off with a bad case of luminous hiccups.

'Not tonight. Tonight, I, G, am in to-tal con-trol,' G told the punch bag as it wobbled and swung on its chain. He turned and surveyed the room.

Everything was just so. Six pens stood like soldiers in a jar. A matching stapler, ruler and hole-punch were lined up at perfect right angles to a notebook. The notebook was dead centre of the desk.

Karate Man must have measured it. G reached for the

ruler to check. Just as he thought . . . sixteen inches and three tenths to the left, sixteen inches and three tenths to the right. What an eejit.

G could have this lot all over the gaff on a count of three. One, two, three . . . he went quite still. He stared at the ruler in his hand and it immediately clattered to the floor.

'Don't let your head get in the way, don't let your head get in the way,' he chanted, almost afraid to hear himself think. He stretched his hand towards one of the pens. He closed his finger and thumb on it. He reached into his mind, as the tae kwon do instructor had described, and visualised.

'I'm lifting the pen, I'm lifting the pen,' he told the darkness. He fought off the urge to clutch at it; he just let the idea of it trickle through his mind.

'Don't let your head get in the way.' Under his breath now.

And the pen was lifting gently into the air. He felt a huge smile spread across his face, chasing the anger away. He heard himself laugh. He had done it. He made himself disappear so that the pen looked as if it was floating on its own above the desk. He reappeared and began to carry it across the room, slowly.

'Who's a clever boy, then?' A voice rasped just above G's head and the pen slipped through his fingers. He blinked up at the windows high in the wall. One of them was open and a crow was sitting on the sill, silhouetted against the relative brightness of a midsummer's midnight. It cocked its head on one side as if it considered G a rare oddity indeed.

'Where did you learn that trick, my little ghosty-whosty?' The crow's voice cackled dryly through the mill's emptiness.

'You can talk?' G spluttered. 'That's ridiculous. You're just an old crow.'

'Well, that's a good one, coming from you.' The crow chuckled. 'I, at least, have a voice box. You, my dear ladeen, are nothing but a shade. And yet you talk, and I'm not falling off my perch with amazement, now am I?'

'But—'

'Nor am I making rude comments of a personal nature. I happen to be a rather young crow and a fine specimen of my sort, if I do say so myself.' It turned itself fully around on the sill to illustrate its point, fluffing out its blue-black feathers and fanning its wings. The full extent of the bird's wingspan filled the entire window. It folded them up again with a smug caw and turned back to G, its eyes glinting.

'You have very fine penmanship for a ghost, ladeen; a very useful skill, that. Pray, where did you get it?'

'Dunno.' G floated upwards to get a closer look at the talking bird, staying out of reach of its evil-looking beak, even though he knew it couldn't harm him. 'What do you care anyway? Picking up a pen would be as easy as pulling a worm, to you.'

'True, true.' The crow considered this statement thoughtfully. 'But it isn't always convenient to do things oneself. Sometimes a . . . a bird . . . could do with a helping hand, so to speak.' It cackled softly. 'Tell me now, how and when did you die? Painful questions, I'm sure, but I am a very curious crow.' It snickered into its feathers then blinked and regarded G with its head inclined.

G frowned again. He had been dead a long time so he supposed a lot of stuff had changed but surely he would know if crows had learnt to talk? Parrots could, and budgies, but crows? Then from the shadows in his mind he remembered his gran telling him once that when she was a kid her neighbour had taught a wild rook to say, 'Get up to the table, Mabel', and 'Come in for your supper, you big-headed duffer'. It also said 'Useless old coot' but Gran had said it learnt that one by itself.

A rook is just another sort of crow, isn't it? G thought. Anyway, this one is definitely talking and I'll talk to whomever or whatever I choose, so I will.

'I tumbled down a big scrapheap that was out there in the yard. It was 'bout ten years ago. My friends scarpered, left me bleeding to death. Cowards.' G waved a hand airily as if dying was something he did every other day.

'Friends!' cawed the crow. 'Not to be trusted, ladeen. They'll use you when it suits them and leave when it doesn't. Most folks don't like to be inconvenienced and dying is very inconvenient. I should know.'

'How? You're not dead, are you?' G snapped.

'No! Noooooooooo!' the crow drawled. 'But we birds don't get a very long time on this spinning ball. A mere matter of years and then, squawk, it's all over and we are worm-food, slug-slimed and claws in the air. But . . . would you like to know a wee secret, ladeen?'

G nodded.

'Sometimes even an old crow may know more about life and death then the smartest of clever-clogs humans.' The crow leaned forward on his perch. 'Tell me now. Would you like to be alive again?'

'Sure I would.' G caught his breath. 'But what's the use in talking about that? Talking won't make it happen, will it?'

'Crow knows things you don't.' The bird cackled. 'Before you died, ladeen, did you believe in ghosts?'

G considered. 'Not really.'

'And before tonight, did you believe you could lift that pen?' The crow shifted from claw to claw, its cold eyes watching G closely.

'Well, I knew I could move it, belt it across the room. But carry it like that, nah. I didn't think I could.'

'And before tonight, my clever young ghost-a-ma-jig—' the crow's eyes slid slyly to the floor '—did you ever believe you would be having a nice old chat with a fine and dandy, very handsome, gloriously glossy, positively erudite – crow?'

G laughed. 'No.'

'There you are then, my young friend. You mustn't measure the possibilities of this mad old world with your own limited imagination. I knows things, so I do. And I may decide to share them with you sometime ... soon—' G caught the gleam in the bird's eye '—if it's to my advantage.'

'To your advantage?'

'Nothing for nothing, my dear, don't ever fool yourself there. Others will make out they do things for the common good. Pah! Don't believe it, ghosty-whosty boy. Everyone's on the take; that's the way of the world. A favour for a favour is what I have in mind. I know a thing or two about life ... and how to get me some more of it. In return for some help with those lifting skills of yours, well, I might be generous enough to share that knowledge with you.'

G tried to form a look of scepticism on his face but his voice shook with excitement. 'Are you serious? You could give me back my life?'

'In exchange for services rendered, it's a definite possibility. You scratch my back, I'll scritch your itch. Do we have a deal?'

'What would I have to do?'

'All in good time, ladeen. I'll be back soon. Next few days. But I need to know that our little conversation stays strictly between you and me. No blabbing to folk, fowl ... or phantom.' The crow's eyes glittered and it attempted to twist its beak into a smile. 'Can I trust you?'

'Sure.' G dug his hands into his jeans pockets and shrugged. 'I have no friends to tell anyway. Who needs them? Not me. Life, that's what I want. I'll do anything for that. Anything.'

The crow cackled again, turned on the ledge and spread its wings.

'See you soon, ladeen,' it rasped as it lifted away from the sill.

G watched it fly off into the night, then drifted back towards the punch bag and gave it a shove.

Could it really be possible? Could a talking crow

know some secret that would bring G back to life? What would he have to do to learn it? Deep inside him a little voice began to speak. 'Shut it!' snapped G.

A shadow moved in the darkness.

'Hey, Coaly-Cat. Did you see that? What do you think? Should I trust a bird's word?' He snorted at his own joke. 'Dunno, Blot. But what's to lose? Talking crows! Way out!' He laughed loudly and shook his head. 'Ha! I have my own secret now! That lot can have their whirly-gig Timecatcher and their big power source mystery. What's it to me?'

He slammed his fist into the punch bag on his way past.

'Life,' he said, as he went through the wall. 'That's the thing.'

✳✳ 18 ✳✳

*O*n Monday afternoon Jessie ran all the way from school straight to the mill. She didn't even go home to change out of her uniform and collect Duff. She ran past a shiny silver car in the yard and up the steps to the Button Detective Agency, two at a time.

'We've got to get a new plan together,' she said, as she burst through the door. 'G and Master Greenwood could—'

'Jessie! How was school, today?' Jason was suddenly standing right in front of her, blocking her view of the room, pulling faces and making small pointing gestures over his shoulder. Then he pinned a grin on his face and turned back into the room. 'We have a visitor, Jessie. Meet Mr Narls Cunningham. He's thinking of buying the mill from our landlord and he's here to look the place over.'

A skinny man in a big suit was leaning against Nat's desk. He had a measuring tape in one hand and a calculator in the other. Nat was looking up into his face with an expression of polite concern.

'It gets very cold in winters time,' she said. 'Freezing. Terrible draughts, there are. They whistle. And it's damp. All the paper in the office curls. Dark, too. We have to have the lights on all day.'

'Sounds like you detectives could do with moving to a better building, then.' His voice was honeyed but his smile was sarcastic. 'If I buy the mill this will be the room I'll use as my office, so I'm afraid I won't be extending your lease.' He moved away from the desk, turned his back on them and began to measure the wall.

Nat turned to Jason and Jessie and silently threw her arms up. 'Do something!' she mouthed.

'So, Mr Cunningham—' Jason cleared his throat '—what prompted your interest in this building?'

'Oh, like the little girl there, I have a plan.' Narls Cunningham looked back at Jessie and winked. It was a strange, slow, sly wink. Jessie watched his left eyelid dip unhurriedly over his eye and lift again, lizard-like. 'You tell me your plan,' he said to Jessie. 'And I'll tell you mine.'

'I–I–I—' Jessie stuttered in alarm. Quick, think.

'Any chance of a coffee, Jessie?' Jason propelled her towards the kettle. 'I'm parched.'

'A bit young for a summer job, isn't she?' Narls Cunningham raised his eyebrows and turned back to the wall.

'She's his—,' Nat said.

'—sister,' said Jason.

'Niece.' Nat nodded.

'Whatever.' Narls Cunningham was at the bottom of the four steps. He was staring at the bricks above them. He shoved the tape and calculator into his pocket and placed a foot slowly on the bottom step. He began to climb. Jessie held her breath, Nat grew pale and Jason stood quite still. The man reached his hand towards the bricks and caressed them gently. The spoon Jessie was holding clattered to the floor. The noise seemed to wake Cunningham from his reverie.

'Steps that lead nowhere. How intriguing,' he remarked.

'There was a door, apparently,' Jason said. 'They say a man walked through it, on a certain day, and was never seen again.' He looked Cunningham right in the eye.

'So I'm told.' Cunningham held Jason's gaze. 'These little details just add to the charm this place holds for me.' He jumped off the top step, strode quickly across the room and reached for the handle of the back-room door.

'NO!' Jason stepped in front of Cunningham. 'You can't go in there.'

Behind Cunningham's back Jessie and Nat exchanged horrified looks – the timeline, all the information on the Timecatcher, plastered all over the walls – no, he mustn't go in there.

'Your landlord assured me I could look around everywhere.' Cunningham's voice was silky but there was a flicker of annoyance in his hooded eyes.

'We keep a lot of information – about our cases – up on the walls in there, where we can see it and study it,' Jason said firmly. 'Confidential information. I'm afraid I can't give you access to that room, I'm sure you understand.'

'I'm sure I do.' The sarcastic smile again. 'Perfectly.' He moved away from the door and gave a little bow.

Relieved, Jessie leaned down to pick up the spoon she'd dropped.

111

There in the shadows, under the bench, two eyes. Watching her.

'Uff!' She whacked her head against the underside of the counter.

G. His face was level with her knees, his head and shoulders sticking up through floorboards and buttons. The rest of him, presumably, dangling beneath in the kickboxing studio. She smothered her exclamation and he scowled rather pathetically then stuck out his tongue.

'What are you doing?' she whispered.

'Listening!' he hissed. 'I'd have thought that was obvious.'

'You're after frightening the life out of me!' Jessie hissed. 'Stay out of sight.' She straightened up. Narls Cunningham was leaving.

'Thank you for your time,' he said smoothly, shaking Jason's hand. 'Good luck with your plans, little girl,' he said to Jessie, with another slow wink. 'Won't you wish me luck with mine?'

'Er, sure. Good luck,' Jessie mumbled. She crossed two fingers behind her back.

'That's a bit half-hearted!' He laughed and, to Jessie's surprise, his laugh was like a donkey bray. 'He-he-he-haaaw! Never mind, little girl. I don't need luck because mine is one very excellent plan.' And he was gone, sloping down the stairs to the silver sportscar.

Greenwood materialised in a corner.

'Did you hear all that?' Jason asked.

'Every word,' the big ghost said grimly. 'He thinks he can take over the Timecatcher and turn it into a circus. Sully has definitely sold him that idea.'

'What were you going to say when you arrived, Jessie?' asked Nat. 'Something about G and Master Greenwood?'

'Well, we know Narls Cunningham means to get cameras into the Timecatcher and Sully wants to snatch the power source. If Master Greenwood and G work together they could sabotage whatever they do. You know, Master Greenwood uses his holding powers on Sully and G uses his power to move or smash anything Narls tries to put in there . . . G's here, by the way.' She pointed to where G was lurking.

'Hope you're done with thy sulkin' now, boy.' Greenwood looked over at the dark under the counter. 'No more tantrums. Work to do.'

G emerged from under the counter and floated uncertainly in front of Greenwood.

'You told me to get lost last night,' the boy said, half wary, half eager.

'I was angry last night, same as thee. We're all uneasy, what with the portal due to open tomorrow morn' and no knowin' what'll happen next.' Greenwood sighed. 'We need to work together now, all o' us, or we'll achieve nothin'.'

G nodded and shoved his hands into his jeans pockets.

Jessie turned back to the kettle and smiled to herself. That's better, she thought.

An inky shadow slid through the bricks and poured itself from the counter to the floor.

'Hi, Blot.' Jessie gathered up the mugs as the kettle began to roar. The cat ignored her, heading straight to Greenwood. Tail up, she threaded herself between and through the big ghost's ankles, left, right, left, right. Greenwood smiled. Then frowned. The frown became a scowl. He rounded on G who was leaning over Nat's shoulder watching her type. Suddenly the boy was being yanked backwards and spun around. Greenwood raised his hands and G shot upwards, arms out, as if he was chained to some invisible beam just below the ceiling. Jason sprang to his feet, knocking over his chair. Jessie stepped forward.

'You weasel!' Greenwood shouted. 'You wretch!' He was so furious his eyes were bulging and some spittle gathered on his beard. 'You've been plottin' with our enemy, you traitorous little worm! You've been talkin' to Sullivan Ellz'mede!'

✳✶ 19 ✶✳

Greenwood had grown to enormous proportions, his anger swelling him until he had to bend his head to keep it out of the attic above. He was glaring at G, green eyes blazing at the suspended boy. Below them Jason was clearly shocked and Nat and Jessie looked anxious.

'Tell them!' roared the irate ghost. 'Tell them what you've done, Pooka-boy!'

G wriggled furiously in the air. What the hell? he thought frantically. What's he on about?

Sure, he'd gone and blown it yesterday, smashing up Painterman's studio. But afterwards he'd cooled down, realised the ring business wasn't anyone's fault and that he was acting like a spoilt kid. The talking crow with its daft promises had weirded him out a bit but today he just wanted back in with Greenwood and Jessie and the detectives. The last few days had been the best ever. New friends, stuff to do. He'd skulked under the counter top simply to be close to the action and, suddenly, Greenwood seemed to have decided to trust him again. But that had only lasted for an eye blink. Now here he was, screaming rubbish at G like some old nutter.

'Speak, you little toad!' yelled Greenwood. He had turned a violent purple.

This just wasn't fair! Anger and disappointment had

a little tussle in G's chest. Anger won. He blinked back the stupid tears that had welled up in his eyes. That crazy crow was right about one thing, he thought. Friendship is for eejits.

'I done nothing!' G shouted, right into Greenwood's face. 'I'm saying nothing.' He clamped his mouth shut. This seemed to infuriate Greenwood even more. He moved his arms as if to fling the boy out through the roof, out of the building completely. Out.

'Stop it!' Jason's voice shook. 'Put him down. Now.'

Greenwood looked at Jason then lowered his arms without warning. For a moment G was a live boy once more, dropping from a height in a falling dream, falling from a sliding car before everything went black. Then he was in control again and he caught himself up with a jerk. He attempted a dignified landing on the floor and almost made it. One foot was standing inside Nat's handbag. He slid it out nonchalantly, then slouched against the wall and dug his hands into his pockets. He pulled his chin down to his chest and let his fringe fall across his face. The tears were back again.

'Tell them,' Greenwood said quietly, shrinking back to his normal size. 'Tell them what you've done.'

Snot was threatening to snivel down his lip now. G sniffed it back up and, to cover the sniff, began to yell.

'I done nothing! I've never met Sully Ellz'mede, you looney; he's probably just a crazy old liar, like you. You're making all of this up as you go along, aren't you? Now it's nearly showtime and when that wall stays just a wall and nothing happens at dawn tomorrow, except the sun coming up, everyone's going to know the 'catcher stuff is all a pack of lies. You're going to look like the barmy old fool you are, so you're just trying to make a show of me, to take the heat off of you. You're a nutter, a complete nutter. Go to hell.'

'Okay, G, enough! Calm down.' Jason's voice wasn't unkind. He turned to Greenwood. 'What makes you accuse G of speaking to Sullivan Ellz'mede? A moment ago you were allowing him back in on things; what's changed?'

Greenwood leaned down towards the floor and gathered up an armful of inky blackness. The ghost cat began to purr and a shadow rippling near Greenwood's chin suggested she was rubbing her head along his beard.

'Blot told me.' Greenwood didn't bother looking up; he went on stroking the cat. G snorted. He could see the expressions on the others' faces. Jason blinked, rubbing his chin with his knuckles. Nat's eyebrows shot skyward and Jessie's mouth fell open, as it always did when she was surprised.

Greenwood shrugged. 'She's shown me many things over the years, has Blot. She has a gift from her years in the Timecatcher, just like I do. Bein' trapped in there with the power source has given her her own wee bit o' magic. She walks through you and you get pictures in thy head, pictures o' things she has seen during her travels around the mill, pictures o' her thoughts. You see what she's seen, you know what she knows.'

G saw Jason and Nat glance at each other. Jessie looked confused. He wished she'd look at him. Say something. He could see no one was sure what or who to believe any more. They couldn't be serious? They must see Greenwood was a fraud now. One minute all friendly and steady, next minute, raging and crazy. He was losing it. G had believed in Greenwood too, believed his story. He'd believed it so hard. He'd tried acting like it was probably a load of rubbish and that he didn't care anyway, but he did. He wanted there to be a Timecatcher and a portal-thing that opened every seven years. He wanted to believe that there was a great adventure to be had and that, he, G, was going to be part of it.

It had all been a fantastic lie. The disappointment set G sniffing again. Inside his head, pain and anger. Red on red. He's going to be thrown out and this time it really isn't fair.

Greenwood sets Blot back on the floor. Says nothing, just strokes her and points her towards Jessie. What now? The cat flickers through the sunlight, through the bin, around Nat's legs, straight towards Jess in a wave of quick, soft shadow. The shade leaps towards the girl and she instinctively opens her arms to catch the flying darkness; the shadow cat passes through her, landing on the counter behind. There she stretches, sits and washes a front paw, oblivious to all the eyes, ghost and living, fixed firmly on her. Or maybe she's just feigning indifference. You never know with a cat.

Now all eyes turn to Jessie. G's head is thumping. She is looking at him, her expression of confusion turning to one of disappointment and distrust. No. No!

'What did you see, Jessie?' Nat asks.

'I saw G.' Jessie, in a small voice, turning her eyes

away from him. 'Talking. With a man, a ghost of a man. A small dark man. Sitting in a window.'

'G?' Nat turns to him.

'No!' G, shaking now. He's given up trying to stem the tears. They are sliding down his cheeks. 'There was no man. I didn't talk to no man. There was no one. I swear, there was no one.' Even as he says it he hears the lie in his own voice. There was someone. The crow. But it doesn't count. They're talking about Sullivan Ellz'mede, not a crow.

'G?' Jason has heard the lie too. They all have.

'No one!' G mutters. 'Only an old bird.'

'A bird?' asks Nat gently. 'You mean a woman?'

'No!' G needs to yell again. Maybe it's knowing they can all see his tears. Maybe it's the way they are all looking at him, the way Jessie is looking at him. Maybe it's the kindness in Nat's voice despite the distrust in her eyes.

'No!' He mimics Nat's accent. 'A bird! A crow! Caw, caw, caw!'

Jason shakes his head. Nat turns away. Greenwood is silent. It is Jessie who says it. She bites her lip and G would swear he can see a tear in her eye. But then he can't see too well through his own.

'Go away, G,' Jessie says. 'Just go away.'

✳✳ 20 ✳✳

*J*essie was staring at a wall again; she was doing that a lot these days. G had gone quietly, just faded into the bricks. She ran her hand under her nose quickly. Nat patted her shoulder.

'I shouldn't have trusted G,' Jessie blurted out. 'I mean, he nearly killed me, for goodness sake. But he seemed so lonely and I kept thinking he'd be okay if only we gave him a chance. Now look what he's done.'

''Tis not thy mistake, lass, 'tis mine.' Greenwood had gathered Blot back into his arms and was staring through the window at nothing at all. 'Bad side always wins out with that boy. I thought maybe this time would be different; I was wrong. Who knows what damage he's done? I should never have let him be part o' this. My choice, my fault.'

Greenwood turned. 'The way to the Timecatcher will be open from dawn tomorrow. I'll be awake day and night till it closes again so I need to get some rest now.' He looked at Jason and Nat. 'I'll see ye at sunrise, then.' He lifted Blot onto his shoulders; she kneaded them briefly with her paws then draped herself around his neck like a shimmering black scarf. Man and cat faded into the air and were gone.

'I really did trust G,' Jessie said in a small voice. 'I still

120

can't believe he's bad. Thoughtless, but not really bad.'

'Talking to Sullivan Ellz'mede, the biggest danger to the stability of the Timecatcher, is beyond thoughtless,' Jason said.

'But maybe G didn't tell him anything. Maybe G was trying to get information out of Sully,' Jessie said, hope making her voice rise. 'We never gave him a chance to explain.'

'We did and he lied,' Jason said curtly. 'If he hadn't done anything wrong he wouldn't have lied about meeting Sully. A crow, he said, for goodness sake.'

'It's a game to the boy ghost, I think,' said Nat, shaking her head. 'He doesn't see how serious protecting the Timecatcher is.'

'But he worked so hard training to hide the ring,' Jessie protested.

Jason shrugged. 'I think he just liked being the centre of attention and when the spotlight was off him he went elsewhere for his fun. No sense of loyalty. There's just no getting away from the truth, Jessie. As Master Greenwood said, we gave him a chance and he blew it.'

Jessie nodded miserably. But? No buts. Go away, G.

'Why did you guys get involved in this?' she asked. 'I mean, how did protecting the Timecatcher become your job?' She sat down and hugged her arms around herself.

Jason leaned forward, linking his hands behind his head and dropping his elbows to his knees. He looked at Nat and she smiled.

'When Greenwood first came through that wall I thought I had to be seeing things. Nat was out of the

121

office at the time; Master Greenwood approached me when I was alone. He was very polite, very patient. Waited for me to calm down a bit. Waited for me to manage a coherent sentence or two. He asked for my help, told me it might be dangerous, that if anything happened to the Timecatcher then me and Nat would be first in the firing line. But once he told me his story, I was hooked.'

'You didn't have to get involved,' said Jessie.

'No.' Jason nodded. 'But I wanted to. People think detective work is exciting but it can be pretty boring a lot of the time. The disturbance of the power source could be catastrophic and I – we – can help prevent it.

'And—' Jason leaned back in his chair and put his hands behind his head '—Master Greenwood has promised to help us with some of our cases after the Timecatcher closes. That will be great. I mean he'll be able to go places we can't, listen to conversations we can't get close to. That should get us back on track with the bread and butter work fairly quickly.'

'Speaking of work, we need to stay focused.' Nat clicked her fingers in front of Jason's nose. 'And you— ' she grinned at Jessie '—need to go home and get your homeworkings done.'

Jason stretched and swung his chair from side to side. 'Yes, Nat's right. Back to work. We're here for the whole night.'

'Really? You're staying here tonight?' Jessie's eyes nearly popped out of her head. She had been in the act of swinging her schoolbag onto her back and it swung wide, catching Jason in the chest.

'Uff!' He caught the bag and held it for her as she threaded her arms through the straps. 'Yes. We need to keep Narls Cunningham out of here; if he's going to try accessing the portal it's likely to be at night. The portal opens tomorrow and the Timecatcher will be vulnerable from then until it closes again at dusk in three days' time, so we're here on duty straight through till Thursday.'

'You'll both be here at dawn when the Timecatcher opens? Oh, I'm so jealous!' Jessie pulled a mournful face then brightened. 'Can I stay tomorrow night? Please? Please, please, please?'

Jason shook his head. 'I don't think your mam would be happy to let you do that, Jessie. What reason could you possibly give her for staying here?'

'I'll think of something. If she says yes, can I?'

'Too dangerous.' He shook his head again, waved, and turned back to his desk.

'Nat?' Jessie was practically begging.

'You work on your mother and I will work on Jason.' Nat dropped her voice to a whisper. 'I'll give you some advice, yez? Keep your story close to the truth; it is the best way to lie. Just like Jason did when he told Narls Cunningham what was in the back room. You understand?'

Jessie laughed. 'I think so. See you tomorrow.'

So later that evening, for the first time ever, she lied to her mam.

'We're doing a project in school,' she said. 'It's called "what I want to be when I grow up".' (True, as it happened.) 'And I'm basing mine on the detectives.' (Also true.)

And, she continued, the detectives had been asked by their landlord to investigate reports of ghost sightings (not true), and they were staying in the mill overnight to check it out (nearly true).

And she and a girl called Geena, from school, could stay overnight as observers (true-ish, though she knew G wouldn't appreciate being morphed into a girl even in a story). Must stop worrying about what G thinks, she told herself. What he thinks doesn't matter any more.

'Please, Mam?' Jessie begged. 'I know there are no ghosts really, I mean Nat and Jason think it's hilarious, but the landlord is going to pay them—' (lie, lie, lie) '—so can I go, please?'

'That mill owner has more money than sense,' Mrs Minahan said, laughing. 'Easy earnings for Nat and Jason. Don't you girls stay awake all night though or you'll be wrecked.'

Jessie hadn't expected her mam to give in so easily, she'd expected to have to do a lot of wheedling and explaining. She had expected a row, but her mam was totally fixated on the lie that was Geena. She was delighted that Jessie finally had a friend in school. Her mam was so excited that Jessie nearly blushed with shame.

'We'll have to have Geena to tea soon. What's she like? Where does she live?'

'Er, I call her G for short,' Jessie stuttered. This lying stuff was getting complicated. 'She's got black hair. Lives with her gran. On Manor Street. So, I can really go? Great!'

Jessie gave her mam a quick hug then claimed she had loads of homework to do (true). She had to get away to her room; she couldn't keep up this lying much longer.

✳✳ 21 ✳✳

$\mathcal{T}$he rat squeezed through the gap and ran swiftly along the wall, its whiskers never breaking contact with the skirting board. It stopped. The smells were intense now. People, dust, food, water, wires, stone. And pee, that of both mouse and rat. All smells it was familiar with; they were the snuff and snivel of its daily existence.

The sandwiches were close by. Or maybe it was a baguette, Sully's favourite. The rat was drooling but it hesitated. It sat up on its haunches and sniffed again.

It had taken Sully a while to accustom himself to the rat's eyesight. Through Ratty's eyes the world was less colourful and more out of focus. Sully knew that there was no danger in this room; he could tell all the blurry shapes were furniture. Even so, he let his rat-host take its time, bobbing its head from side to side. It would move when it was ready.

Over the last month Sully had learned to have some respect for the animal's instincts. Especially since the night of the owl incident. He'd wanted Ratty to cross a road; they'd looked right and left. No cars, no vehicles of any sort, no cats. All clear, go, Ratty, go. But the rodent wouldn't budge and was all for running down a drain. Sully had been quite angry; they'd struggled hard for control of Ratty's wee body, Sully calling his host ten different types of ungrateful fool.

Sully had been angry, but, more than that, he was bitterly disappointed. He'd hand-picked Ratty from its litter, after all, favoured the little runt over its multitude of bigger brothers and sisters, chosen it for his special attention. He expected Ratty's grateful compliance in return and now the long-tailed twit wouldn't even cross a road for him. Sully was exasperated.

'Have it your way, then,' he'd huffed.

Ratty had been down that drain fast. The owl had missed them, but only just. Sully would never forget the view of those huge talons nor how the bird's shadow had momentarily blackened the drain as it silently swept by above them. Poor Ratty shook for a good ten minutes. Sully had apologised profusely.

What a near thing that had been. Sully was aware that while he inhabited an animal's body his spirit was linked with its spirit. He was fairly sure that the death of the animal would mean his death. Again. Of course, he could always leap out of his host before it was killed but only if he saw death coming. Would his spirit survive dying again? Sully wasn't so sure. He might be forced to move on this time. And Sully had no intention of moving on. Moving back held more attraction. Back towards life.

Since the night of the owl, Sully felt closer to Ratty then ever. Ratty trusted him as no other animal host had before. Now Sully trusted Ratty in return – the wee whiskery flea-ball was the son he'd never had. Ratty became less of an 'it' and more of a 'him'.

'Ah! All safe, eh?' Ratty was making his move on the ham sandwich, at last. They moved away from the skirting board and scampered across the floor to a battered briefcase leaning against a table leg. The zip was open, which meant they wouldn't have to do an hors d'oeuvre of leather and lining. Ratty was inside quickly and through the clingfilm in seconds.

Fuff, faff, fuff, thought Sully, as bits of the plastic wrapper went down Ratty's throat. Ah, yes! Ham. Not as good as the Widow Clancy's, mind, and the bread certainly can't hold a candle to Childless Maggie's, but oh, Ratty-boy! It's so good to taste food again.

The Widow Clancy and Childless Maggie, Sully hadn't thought of them in centuries. They'd been like mothers to him, better mothers than his own feckless ma. Like Ratty, Sully had been naturally small and weak as a young fella, while his three brothers had been big bruisers of lads. There wasn't much food to go around, mealtimes were a dash-and-grab affair. Sully usually ended up shoved to the floor, looking up as his brothers scoffed the lot. Sometimes he'd stay where he was and wait for something to drop. Like a dog.

The fight for survival taught Sully to use his wits. By the age of six he had learnt that a cheeky smile and bit of chat could earn him a meal from the local dames, at least those with no kids of their own to feed. The Widow Clancy's only son had gone to sea when he was thirteen and never come home. And Childless Maggie had had three husbands but no wains. Both women doted on Sully and he split his time between them so as not to wear out his welcome with either.

He'd eaten like a king until he was twelve when the Widow Clancy had upped and died and Childless Maggie took herself another husband. Maggie's new husband had seen clean through Sully, taken him aside and told him to clear off. Sharpish.

He left Stoneybatter and Dublinia behind and struck out to try his fortune elsewhere. He'd built himself up a fine repertoire of scams, mainly aimed at the ladies of the towns and villages he visited.

Ah, what fun he'd had. Until he'd come home to Dublinia at the age of five and twenty and tried his luck with a girl by the name of Martha. A fine-looking girl she'd been too. Sully had winkled her family's darkest secrets out of her in no time at all. Then he had set about his usual game, hinting to the girl's father what he knew, while throwing in a mention of his own money problems. Unfortunately Martha turned out to be the niece of the city's justiciar; Sully had suddenly found himself imprisoned, tried for blackmail and sentenced to hang.

But even death hadn't blunted the joy of executing a good scam. Sully had spent some time selecting Narls Cunningham as the target for his latest, his greatest. He needed someone young but wealthy. Someone with a flair for business, but with an ego that would blind him to Sully's real intentions. Someone too clever for his own good, as the saying goes.

'Narls, Narls, Narls.' Sully shook his head in mock despair and Ratty lost a mouthful of crumbs. 'How can you not see what I'm up to, you silly, vain twit? Because you're beguiled by the idea of all the money to be made, eh?' Sully chuckled, causing Ratty to choke on a scrap of clingfilm. 'Cahaa, cahaa!'

'He knows about you and me, Ratty-boy. Kept you in the cage I asked him to get for you. Couldn't go losing you once I'd trained you up all nice and well-behaved.' Sully smiled fondly inside Ratty's head. 'How else could I have gotten into the mill again? Greenwood can sense me as a spectre but not as a little ratty-tatty in Narlsy-Warlsy's pocket.'

Ratty munched contentedly on the last scrap of ham. The hum in his head babbled on. Ratty was used to it, it had been there from the beginning. It rarely left him. It made him feel safe and strong, like a rat with an extra set of whiskers.

'All Greenwood's planning with his gang of little helpers won't stop me,' Sully hissed. 'Ah, Ratty! All that power waiting for me. Just on the other side of that wall. The way in is open, Ratty. Been open since dawn this morning. You and me, we could just slip right in, right now ... but no. We have to wait till tomorrow, the day when the sun shines longest and the magic is strongest. That is the day our plans are most likely to work, Ratty-boy, so Sully will just have to be a patient old spook.' Sully's excitement had set Ratty quivering.

'Calm down, Flea-ball, finish your dinner. Don't worry, Sully knows his way about in there. Greenwood will never know I'm in the Timecatcher as long as I'm with you. The daft eejit's too busy looking for some silly old ring, anyway; he thinks that's where the power is. But you and me know better, Ratty. We'll be scampering through the centuries on your little ratty claws and we'll grab the Spark and be out of there with it clutched between your large front teeth before Greenwood ever knows I was there. You just have to aim yourself where Sully points you. I can't do it without you, Ratty-boy. How else will I do what I want to do but inside my dear wee rat?'

Sully relaxed while Ratty began to clean his whiskers; it was rather a pleasant ritual. 'Well, actually, there is another way. You are Plan A, Ratty-boy. I just know those sharp quick claws of yours will manage that vortex, no problem. It should be just like running up and down curtains to you. I suppose there's an itty-bitty chance you might lose your grip and fall, so now I have that Ghosty-Whosty boy in my sights for Plan B. If you can't manage the Timecatcher and the precious magical thing, he can. A few empty promises and he'll do whatever I ask. One way or another, tomorrow I'll have the Spark.' He smiled to himself.

'Narls Cunningham. I'll have to get used to my new name, Ratty-boy, and he'll have to get used to his new brain. When I have the Spark he'll only be an occasional whisper in the back of his own head.

'Silly man! He knows I can become you, Ratty-boy, knows I have big plans for you, but it never occurs to him that I might have even bigger plans for him. Plans that don't involve this reality TV stuff he's so excited about, har har. Cahaa, cuffaw! Bloomin' plastic!'

✳✳ 22 ✳✳

*J*essie wobbled slightly on the doorstep grabbing armfuls of sleeping bag as the blue nylon threatened to slide away from her. She should have put it into something, but she was in a hurry. It was Tuesday, and the portal to the Timecatcher would be open. She had run home from school. Again. Now she was trying to get out of the house as fast as she could, before her mam started asking more questions. She bundled the sleeping bag under one arm and she and Duff were at the bottom of Sitric Street by the time Mrs Minahan appeared at the door, calling after them.

'Hold on a sec, Jess, I want to talk to you about this overnight thing.' Her mam looked anxious, even from this distance, but Jessie pretended not to hear her right.

'Yeah, thanks, bye,' she called over her shoulder and turned the corner at a run. The sleeping bag unravelled and tripped her up a minute later. Well, that's what you get for telling lies to your ma, Jessie Minahan.

In the mill yard, she hooshed up the slippery sleeping bag yet again and half-ran, half-hobbled up the stairs to the Button Detective Agency door. She grabbed the door handle but the door stayed firmly shut.

'Who is it?' Nat's voice came sing-song from inside the office.

'Me, Jessie,' Jessie called impatiently. 'And Duff.'

She heard footsteps and a key turning. The door opened and Nat beckoned her inside. 'We're keeping it locked, for safety reasons,' she whispered, and closed the door behind Jessie again.

'Does that mean—' Jessie stared at the wall above the steps '—it's open? The way to the Timecatcher is really open?'

Jason leapt up from his computer. 'The portal opened with the rising sun, just like Master Greenwood said it would!' He grinned and beckoned Jessie towards the back wall, his face alive with excitement. Nat scooped Duff up in her arms and followed them. 'Master Greenwood went in right away to begin his search for the ring and we haven't heard anything from him yet.'

They all stopped in front of the steps and Jason stood behind Jessie with his hands on her shoulders. She looked at the bricks. They were all there, as brick-like as usual. She turned to Jason, puzzled. 'It looks just like it always does,' she said.

'Stand still a moment,' he said. 'Can you feel the pull?'

She waited and, sure enough, something was faintly tugging at her clothes and the laces of her runners were twitching. One strand of her hair floated out from her face towards the wall, then another, then another, and soon she was gazing at the bricks through a veil of her own dark hair. Her skin was prickling. The past was behind that wall, through those bricks. She lifted her foot towards the first step.

'Oh no you don't!' Jason gripped her shoulders tighter. 'You have to be careful or the Timecatcher will pull you in. I had a look inside this morning; didn't dare do more than stick my head in. It took all my strength to keep my balance and pull myself back out of there.'

'And then he held onto me so I could have a look.' Nat's voice was full of wonder.

'What did you see?' Jessie gasped.

'Swirlings!' replied Nat. 'Bright light. Everything was a mass of spinning waves. Like water, but not water. Like how I imagine it would be inside a tornado.' She shook her head in wonder and cuddled Duff, who was whining anxiously.

'Wow!' Jessie could hardly speak. She had believed Greenwood when he said there was a portal, of course she had. But believing it in her head and seeing it with her own eyes were two different things. Now it was here, really here. She could feel it calling to her. 'Please,' she said. 'Please, can I—'

'No way! Sorry, Jess, the pull is too strong. Too dangerous. What would I tell your mam, eh? The wall *ate* you?'

'But if you held onto me like you did with Nat—'

Jason wouldn't budge. He wouldn't let Jessie near the wall, let alone touch it.

Jessie was still trying to persuade him when Nat gave a strange, strangled squeak. Jason and Jessie stared at her. She seemed to be choking. Her eyes were round and horrified. Duff was squeaking too and struggling furiously in her arms. Nat held onto him with one hand and used the other to point shakily past Jason and Jessie, back at the wall they had just stepped away from.

'Nat? You okay?' asked Jason, turning to see what she was pointing at.

'Rat!'

'What?'

'Rat!' Nat closed her eyes. 'In the corner. A rat! Huge! It was sitting there watching us.'

Duff wriggled free, jumped to the floor and raced to the wall, sniffing furiously.

'We have to sleep here tonight,' Nat groaned. 'With a rat!'

'Pizza,' said Jason firmly. 'We've been cooped up in here all night and day. Time for some grub and a change of venue. Both of you, my treat. Come on. Duff will keep the rats out.'

'What about Narls Cunningham?' asked Jessie. 'What if he tries to get at the portal while we're not here?'

'I doubt he'll try to break in in broad daylight,' Jason said. 'I think Duff would give him hell if he tried. And—' he jangled his keys '—I've added an extra lock, so he'd have to actually break the door down.'

Nat fished a biscuit out of the tin and tossed it to the terrier. He swallowed it in one go and turned his back on them, sat down and gazed intently at a small hole in the skirting board. He was almost perfectly still, just a wee quiver running through his stocky frame.

'He will be our guard dog tonight, Jessie?' Nat grabbed Jessie's hand. 'He is a good rat-dog, yez?'

'Duff is a great ratter, Nat.' Jessie tried not to wince;

Nat's nails were long and she was squeezing Jessie's hand too tight. 'Pizza sounds good, let's go.'

She tugged Nat towards the door. Jason hooked his mobile onto his jeans and they all stepped out into the sun-lit yard.

✳ ✳ 23 ✳ ✳

'A little fun to while away the day, Ratty-boy. It's just a game, my lad, making people squeal and jump, no need for your tiny heart to thump so. The doggy wasn't going to get you. I wouldn't let that happen to my Ratty-Tatty.'

They had scarpered from the detectives' rooms, sharpish. Now they were in the corridor that led to the artists' studios. Ratty shivered on a sunny windowsill. The blurred figures of the detectives and the girl had just left the yard. It was empty for all of two minutes when a new blur entered. A woman, Sully guessed. She walked over to the back stairs, up to the Button Detective Agency door, and knocked.

After a moment the woman turned and headed back down into the yard where she hesitated and looked up at the first floor windows. Sully drew Ratty's head back from the glass.

'Hello? Hello?' The woman's voice drifted upwards.

The grate and dong of footsteps on metal stairs, coming closer. Ratty jumped down from the sill and slipped back into the shadows at the end of the corridor.

'Jessie? Are you there?' The blur stepped through the door and was looking around.

Nearby a door opened and a new blur emerged into the corridor. A man.

'Hi. You okay? Can I help you?'

'My daughter, Jess. I'm looking for her. I don't suppose . . .?'

''Fraid I haven't seen Jessie today.'

'You know her?'

'She helped me clean up my studio the other day, after a . . . a break in.'

'Did she? She's not in your way? I mean, I know she's hanging out here a lot. I just don't want her being a nuisance to anyone.'

'She's not in my way. Something wrong? You want help finding her?'

'No. I – I'm just being silly, really. Fussing about nothing. And she hates that.'

'If you're sure,' the man said.

'Are you one of the painters?' the woman asked.

'Well, I'm trying to be. Have a few paintings on the go. Would you like to see them? Only, I could do with someone else's opinion.'

'Sure.' The woman's voice relaxed a little. 'Yes. Why not?' She came down the corridor to the man's studio.

'Sure, why not?' Sully said inside Ratty's head and scurried in around the door jamb, unnoticed.

The woman admired the room, the neatness and order, admired the old stone walls, then made polite noises about the paintings. She said they were, em, 'interesting'.

'Interesting?' Sully spluttered. 'They're grey. Grey on grey. Muddy grey, rainy grey, mouldy grey. They couldn't be more boring if he'd gone and left the canvas completely blank. People, my dear Ratty, so often feel compelled to be polite. It would do this deluded eejit more good if yer woman just told it like it is: "your paintings stink, deary, they're useless rubbish."'

Sully skulked around the skirting board for a bit. All this waiting around was getting to him, Ratty's incessant need to remain in the shadows was getting to him, the blasted skirting boards were getting to him.

The pull of the Timecatcher was getting to him.

He wanted to enter it now, this minute, even though he knew it wasn't the right time. He had to stick to his plan. He had waited seven long years.

'Another day, Sully, you can do it,' he scolded himself.

But with the portal open now he could feel the Timecatcher, its power seeping out, oozing through the building, calling to him. He'd followed the woman into this room in search of some fresh diversion only to find he had chosen to earwig on the two dullest people in Dublin.

'Gawd, Ratty! I'm so bored I think we'll have to find a hole in the wall and have a good old kip, for want of something better to do. What's become of people, Ratty? I'd swear they were more interesting in my day. This lot are like a load of old boots: all tongue, no soul, har har har! Geddit, Ratty-boy? Oh, I guess not, you pink-toed plonker.'

Sully rolled his eyes and Ratty twitched anxiously. The wee creature didn't like this constant proximity to humans. He especially didn't like it when the voice in his head made his eyes twirl.

'What are they on about now? Death? Phiff! What do they know about death? Mr Greypaint thinks he has a handle on death just because he dresses in black and paints depressing pictures, does he? Give me strength! Wait, though! What was that? What did he say, Fur-brain? Oh my!'

Ratty began to quiver. The voice was making his brain hot. He tried to draw himself down, flat onto the dusty floor. Stay still, be invisible. Movement draws notice and notice is bad. But the voice wasn't listening to Ratty now, it was booming with excitement. Ratty could do nothing as it overwhelmed all his senses, took complete control of his claws and waltzed them out into the middle of the room.

The middle of the room! Full sunlight, full view, total exposure on all sides. Ratty tried to signal his panic to the voice but the voice was shouting and ranting and Ratty's little brain pulsed fit to explode.

'Wah-hah! Yeh-hey! What a break, Ratty, what luck!' Sully decided a wee jig was in order. 'Hop two, three, four, five, six, seven and a one-two-three and a one-two-three!' Ratty skipped along the floor on his hind legs. The two blurs stopped talking; there were two sharp intakes of breath. They were staring straight at Ratty now, whiskers away, but Sully didn't care.

'Round the house, skip, hop, skip, hop!' Sully was ecstatic! This was amazing; he couldn't have planned it better. In fact, he hadn't planned it better.

'Plan A is ditched, Plan B is botched, on to Plan C! Way-hey! We can't fail with Plan C, Ratty-boy, it's made-to-measure! Move over, Narls Cunningham, the grey painter is my only man!'

Ratty cartwheeled helplessly around the room. Sully guffawed loudly inside the creature's brain. He halted the cartwheeling and stood still for a moment, tipping Ratty's head to one side as he considered the man towering above them.

'No more torturing paintbrushes for you, Georgy-Porgy. Tomorrow you'll be a new man. You and me have a beautiful future together. And, as for the ghosty boy, well, I just knew I'd find a good use for him. I could feel it in my whiskers! Come on, Ratty! A leap, a hop, a plié just for good measure, twirl to finish, and – as we have an audience, Ratty, old son – a bow!'

The two big blurs sucked breath again and stepped quickly backwards from the madly squeaking, hyperactive rodent cavorting at their feet.

'No applause? No cries of "encore"? Well, we'll not stay where we are not appreciated, Ratty-toes! One-two-three, skirting board and – exit, stage left!'

✳✳ 24 ✳✳

'*A*m in the mill,' read the text from Jessie's mam. 'Where u?' It had been sent forty minutes ago.

Drat, thought Jessie.

She had switched her phone back on as she and the detectives were turning back into the yard. This wasn't good. If Jason and her mam came face to face all her lies would be rumbled. Jason had been so distracted by the portal and seeing the vortex, he was easily persuaded to let Jessie stay over. He hadn't actually asked her what she had told her mam but he wouldn't be happy if he realised Jessie only got permission because Mam thought another girl from school would be there too. Even though lies were his business Jessie was pretty sure that this was the sort he wouldn't approve of.

As they walked under the archway, she lagged behind. Just a second longer in the shade, another moment to figure out what to do. No sign of Mam at the top of the steps or in the yard but she must be here somewhere.

Don't panic, she thought. Wait. Pretend to be reading a poster on the gate. That's it. Let Nat and Jason go ahead. And now Nat's looking back to see where I am. Wave . . . smile . . . read poster. 'Over-sixties Bingo club, Thursday nights, 7.30 to 9.30.'

At least if Nat and Jason made it back to the office

before her mam appeared, Jason wouldn't need to know about her deceit.

'Up the stairs, you guys, and safely inside,' she prayed under her breath. 'That's it. In you go. Close the door. Yes! That's Jason out of the way, phew!' The pizza suddenly felt like a heavy wodge of congealed cardboard in her stomach.

Note to self: Lying plus pretending equals indigestion.

If her mam was still here what was she going to tell her? That 'Geena' had been sent home sick from school and couldn't stay in the mill tonight? Not bad, actually.

Mam will insist I go home with her, which will be a real pain, but at least I won't have wrecked everything, she thought. Wow! She shook her head in surprise. For someone who doesn't like lying, you're getting really good at it, Jessie Pants-on-Fire Minahan.

She took a deep breath and walked out of the archway into the sunshine.

'Jessie!'

She swung around. George McCabe was standing just inside the yard, leaning against the bins. He looked odd outside in the light. His skin was very white; she hadn't noticed that before. With the black clothes and hair he resembled a skinny badger. He squinted at her and put a hand up to shade his eyes. The other hand held a large brown paper bag.

'This is for you,' he said, holding it out to her.

'Oh, thanks.' Her hands closed around it without thinking; she was checking out the front staircase for signs of her mother.

'Your ma left it for you.'

'My ma? Oh, right, great. She's gone then?' Jessie said hopefully.

'Yeah. She texted you. You didn't answer.'

'No. Well, I had my phone turned off. We were in the pizza place, me and the detectives.' Jessie turned to go.

'Em . . .' George shoved his hands deep into his jeans pockets and scuffed the ground with the toe of his shoe.

Jessie waited. 'Yes?'

'Your ma.'

'Yes?'

'She's, eh, she's a bit anxious.'

'Yeah, she's always like that. I wouldn't worry if I were you.' She heard the sharpness in her voice and flushed. But up there in the detective offices a portal was open in a brick wall and she hadn't given up on persuading Jason to let her see inside it. Not by a long shot.

'She's sad.' George fiddled with his fringe. 'Your ma. She's lonely.'

'She said that to you?' Jessie swallowed hard.

'No.' George examined the cement at his feet with a frown. 'It's in her voice. It's in the way she walks.'

Jessie opened her mouth and closed it again. This strange man was talking about her mother as if he knew more about her than she did. She knew Mam was sad but she didn't want to think about it now. Her head was full of the Timecatcher. And G, despite what he'd done. There wasn't time to be thinking about Mam as well.

'Your ma thinks G is a girl,' George McCabe said, suddenly looking her straight in the eye.

'You didn't tell her—'

'That he's a boy? A dead boy? No, I didn't tell her.'

'Right. Thanks.' Jessie chewed her lip and looked down at the brown bag in her hands.

'Enjoy your midnight feast, so.' George nodded towards the bag. ''S what that is. Goodies for you and G. From your ma.'

'Right.' Jessie clasped the bag tightly and turned away. She plodded up the back stairs. George was right, Mam was lonely. But the Timecatcher would be closed in a few days. She'd think about her mam then.

** 25 **

'What'zit?' A noise?

Jessie tried to rub her eyes awake but her arms were caught inside her sleeping bag. She wriggled one hand free, pushed her hair back from her face and looked around in the dark. Duff was lying heavily on her feet and Nat was asleep. She and Nat had created a nest for themselves on the floor, making a large circle inside the buttons and filling it with clothes from the back room. Now the musty old-clothes smell was making Jessie want to sneeze.

The office furniture came into focus as she blinked herself more awake. The standby lights on the computers glowed softly, turning everything grey-blue; she could see the whole room quite well.

Had she heard a noise? She tried to grab at the echo of it sliding away into some deep recess of her brain. Nothing.

Nothing, that pretty much summed up the evening at the mill. She'd begged Jason to let her look into the Timecatcher but he was having none of it. He let her help out with some photocopying and by ten fifteen she and Nat had bunked down on the office floor and Jason was snoring in the back room.

It was odd that what should have been the most

exciting day yet had turned out to be the dullest. She couldn't help thinking that it would have been more fun if G was here.

This isn't about having fun, Jessie Minahan, it's about protecting the Timecatcher, she told herself crossly. And G is a traitor to our cause. Now, go back to sleep.

But there it was again, the noise. She hadn't imagined it. She fought with the sleeping-bag zip and wriggled herself halfway out, tipping Duff awake with her feet at the same time. He rose up quickly, regarding her in the gloom. His head flicked to his right and he stared intently over at the portal wall.

'There is something, isn't there?' She struggled the rest of the way out of the bag, wobbled upright and stepped carefully over Nat, trying not to slide on buttons, clearing them quietly with her toes before committing to each small stride across the room.

At the steps she could hear a faint whirring sound which grew louder as she listened. In front of her eyes the central bricks began to pulse and glow.

'Nat,' Jessie whispered. 'Nat, something's happening to the wall.'

The glowing circle grew larger as she watched and the bricks swam outwards towards her, bulging as if a huge wave was about to break through them. A great grey blob loomed, an enormous hand came through the bricks, reaching out towards Jessie's throat.

'Nat!' Jessie could only manage a strangled squeak as she lurched backwards.

'Leave her sleep, lass.' Greenwood raised a finger to his lips as he stepped through the portal into the room.

147

The bricks wavered in the air; he was surrounded by a halo of light. Behind him, Jessie could see a great heaving mass, spiralling inwards like a neon hurricane. The air around her tugged fiercely at her, like a fast retreating tide and she braced her legs to keep her balance. Duff's nose pressed hard against her ankles as he too fought the pull. Then the bricks spun back into place and the wall closed itself abruptly behind Master Greenwood. The room was dark again.

'I can't stay long,' Greenwood whispered, turning himself from dark to low-glow. 'Just here to let ye folk know what's goin' on. You can pass on message t'others in mornin' when they awake.'

'Of course.' Jessie nodded. This was more like it! Midnight messages from the Timecatcher. She looked at her watch.

'What time is it?' asked Greenwood, observing her glance.

'It's two thirty-five am,' she said. 'Do the shadow days keep the same time as real days?'

Greenwood nodded quickly. 'Aye. Whatever time 'tis here, the Timecatcher days are all set the same.'

'Have you found the Ring of Tomar? Is that the message?' Jessie whispered eagerly.

'Aye. I've been workin' my way towards it from either end o' September, in that year we spoke o' before.' He peered around the room uneasily. 'One day, at dawn, the ring's not there, next day there is a shadow o' it, glintin' at me under the dead leaves on the tree-trunk floor.'

'A shadow of it? But where's the real ring?'

'In the day before that shadow appears. I just need to watch that day and, sometime between dawn and midnight, the ring will show itself.'

'But you've seen a shadow of it?' Jessie was thrilled. 'What's it like?'

''Tis half hid, but big and lovely from what I can see.'

'And which day is it in, exactly?' Jessie asked.

'Walls have ears hereabouts so I won't tell thee which, beggin' thy pardon, Jessie, lass.' He glanced around again. 'Himself could be listenin' as we speak.'

'G?'

'Sullivan Ellz'mede.'

'You think Sullivan Ellz'mede is here?'

'He's here, nothin' surer. Can't sense him, like usual, but I know he's here all the same. He's found some way to mask himself from me.'

'What if he's in there already?' Jessie asked, looking at the portal wall.

'He may well be but he won't make a move till after dawn sometime. Tomorrow's when magic in the Timecatcher is strongest, when the ring will be most powerful. Whatever he's plannin' to do, he'll do it 'tween sunrise and sunset.'

'Do you think G—' Jessie hesitated '—is working with him now?' She crossed two fingers behind her back.

Greenwood frowned. 'I'm not sure what G can do to help Master Ellz'mede but Sully'll certainly make use o' him if he can. Usin' other folk is Sully's way.'

Jessie looked around her nervously. None of the

ghosts she'd met these last few days scared her. Greenwood had at first, but not for long. G – well, for all his tricks, she didn't really think ghosts when she thought of G. She thought boy, annoying boy, sad boy. She had even begun to think friend. But Sullivan Ellz'mede was another story. She shivered.

Suddenly Greenwood leaned down and whispered in her ear. '13th o' September, that's where 'tis. Go to sleep again, Jessie, lass. I'll go back in to the Timecatcher to guard the ring as best I can. Stand away off a bit while I go.'

He raised his forefinger to his lips, smiled at her, and turned towards the portal. Jessie grabbed Duff's collar and backed up to the opposite wall. Greenwood floated forwards and the bricks whirred and shifted, the portal gaped. It surrounded and swallowed him with a sucking, popping noise, and he was gone. Jessie half expected the bricks to belch.

Everything was quiet and dark again. The wall at the top of the redundant steps appeared as solid as ever.

'I'll just ...' Jessie knew she shouldn't, she had promised Jason she wouldn't, but now that she had caught a glimpse inside the Timecatcher she wanted to see more. She could feel it tugging her gently, beckoning.

She placed her left foot on the bottom step. Her right foot shuffled onto the next one. She stopped there, two steps from the top. She looked at the bricks. She knew she mustn't ... but the tugging had become a strong pull. The past was just on the other side of the wall. People from the past. Her dad. She reached out her hand. Her whole arm was shaking, the hairs rising along it. Duff was padding anxiously at the bottom of the steps, whining softly.

I won't actually touch it, she thought. I'll just run my hand a centimetre from the surface, see if I can sense the portal through my fingers.

She took a deep breath and reached her fingers closer to the wall.

Closer.

Closer.

Too close! Suddenly her hand was engulfed in brick, her wrist was being gripped in what felt like an intense Chinese burn, her arm was disappearing even as she fought to pull it back. She grabbed at the adjoining wall with her left hand, groping helplessly as she tried to brace her toes against the top step. The wall was taking her in, swallowing her and she couldn't stop it. Her right arm was already inside all the way up to her shoulder. She turned her head away frantically as the side of her neck and then her right ear entered the wall. The faint whirring suddenly became a crazy crashing roar. In her other ear she could just make out Duff barking. All she could see in the grey light were the bricks of the adjoining wall and her free hand scrabbling at them helplessly.

This is the last thing I'm ever going to see. The words flickered through her brain. She heard a hysterical laugh in the distance. Hers?

Is that the best you can do, Jessie Minahan? Laugh as you die? Do something, you eejit! she thought furiously. This wall's all you've got, hold onto it.

Her fingers scraped its surface as the Timecatcher exerted a stronger hold on her. Then she saw it, an old nail lodged between two bricks, sticking out several centimetres, rusty and crooked. Her left hand closed on it and it bit into her palm.

One, two, three, she counted, and heaved, clinging to the nail, bracing her feet against the step and pulling with all her strength. The portal released her just as the nail came away in her hand and she tumbled backwards, down the steps, over Duff, crashing against the filing cabinet. It shuddered. Its open drawers shook some files loose and they spilled their contents over Jessie's head.

'Yez?' Nat sat up quickly and blinked. 'What is going on? Why is Duff growling?'

Jessie scrambled to her feet. She knew Nat was blind as a bat right now; her contact lenses were sitting in their overnight case on the desk.

'Em, it's okay, Nat,' she whispered. 'Duff just wants out for a pee. Sorry for waking you, go back asleep.'

'Why are you over there?' Nat's voice was gravelly and slurred. 'Door's other way.'

'Duff's confused. I'll take him out, don't worry.' Jessie tried to sound soothing. She didn't want Jason waking and coming from the back room and seeing the state she was in – covered in dust and scrapes. He'd guess what she'd done pretty quickly and he'd be angry. He'd have every right to be. She grabbed Duff's collar and walked him towards the office door. On the way past the desk she grabbed keys and her mam's paper bag of treats.

'Back in a minute,' she whispered cheerily. Nat

flopped back down onto her makeshift pillow.

Outside on the top of the back stairs Jessie let the cool air flow over her as she tried to steady her breathing. Duff glared up at her with one eye, the other hidden behind his yellow-grey fringe.

'Sorry, Duffer.' She squatted down and threw her arms around his neck. 'That was probably the stupidest thing I've ever done, I'm sorry I scared you.'

She buried her face in his fur and gave one shaky sob. Careful Jessie, that's what her old friends in Kilkenny used to call her. She always thought things through, she never made snap decisions. What had got into her these last few days? Snap, snap, lie, snap. Duff pressed his nose into her cheek and licked her ear, then pulled away and raced down the stairs, wagging his stumpy tail.

Jessie laughed and wiped a grimy hand across her eyes. The yard below was a tangle of shadows and moonlight. Duff stood in the centre of it looking up at her, lolling his tongue out in a dog laugh, waiting for some new fun to begin. She lifted the goody bag in her hand. Chocolate! That would help her recover.

'Time for a midnight feast, Duff?' She started down the stairs after him.

✳✳ 26 ✳✳

*D*uff didn't wait for Jessie to reach the ground; he turned, bounded up the other stairway and stood, panting, at the door to the studio corridors.

'Come back down, Duff, come on,' Jessie whispered from the middle of the yard. She rattled the brown bag of sweets and treats in the air. 'Look what I have.'

He didn't turn his head, instead he began furiously scratching at the metal stairs, *scraaach*, *scraach*, like fingernails down a blackboard. Jessie padded quickly up the steps and grabbed his collar.

'Stop it, Duff. Door's locked. Look,' she said, pushing it clumsily with her goody-bag hand.

It swung inwards. Duff wriggled out of her grip and padded happily into the corridor, following some vital scent only he could detect.

'It's that rat again, I suppose.' Jessie rolled her eyes and followed him in, hugging the bag to her chest. To her surprise there was light shining out from under a door and a faint thump, thump of rock music in the background. George McCabe was working late. Your ma, she's lonely, he'd said.

'Let's go, Duff. I can't face him right now.'

But Duff had already trotted around the corner into the other corridor. She followed. White moonlight streaming through the windows had turned that corridor a cold blue-white, hatched with inky shadows spidering across the floor and up the walls. The windows of this corridor stretched almost from floor to ceiling. The big metal doorway G had tried to push her out of the other day was closed now, chopping the light in two. The far end of the corridor was pitch black. Duff darted away, disappearing in the dark. Jessie stepped into the light of the first window where she had a good view of the yard below and the moon hanging behind the Button Detective Agency roof. The window ledge was deep; it would make a decent seat. She began to unload the contents of the brown bag.

Two of everything: two cans of red lemonade, two packets of crisps, two bars of chocolate, two apples. Jessie bit her lip. All her favourite things. All her mam had got in return was a text which read 'thx 4 d treats'. Jessie flopped down on the windowsill and picked up a can. The noise of the ring pull parting company with the lid seemed to crash down the corridor like a wave. She took a slurp; the lemonade was lukewarm.

Should have put it in Jason's mini-fridge, she thought, shoving a square of chocolate into her mouth.

She tried to open the crisps quietly, tugging gently on the packet to make it open slowly but it exploded suddenly like a Christmas cracker and crisps tumbled out onto the floor. She stifled a giggle.

'Duff! Crisps,' she whispered into the shadows. Where had he got to? Usually the mere rattle of a crisp bag would bring him running. She pulled her feet up onto the ledge and hugged her knees to her chest.

May as well enjoy the moon, she thought.

The glass in the window was old and thick. The surface was warped and, depending on which bit of the pane she looked through, the world outside was still and clear, or milky-fuzzy. She began to sway from side to side, making the mill roofs stretch and shrink, the moon swim and shimmer. She laughed.

Then froze.

The hair prickled along the back of her neck. Eyes. Eyes in the window, watching her. Just for a moment she saw a face.

A man, a small, skinny, dark-haired man.

Just like the man Blot had shown her.

Sullivan Ellz'mede.

Smirking.

She swung around. There was nothing behind her and when she looked back at the glass there was nothing there either. She jumped up, knocked over the drink can and stepped on the fallen crisps. Clanks and crunches echoed in the emptiness.

'Duff! Duff!' she hissed into the darkness. 'Come here, boy, I need you. Please, Duffer!' She could feel her heart hammering. Breathe, Jessie.

Where was Duff? Why wasn't he coming when she called? She forced herself to stand still and listen. She couldn't hear him. No padding paws, no nails clicking on floorboards, no snuffling. She began to walk slowly along the corridor, her eyes avoiding the windows.

Why couldn't I just stay in my sleeping bag? She sighed. 'Duff!'

Jessie reached the hulking black shadow of the big

door and walked through it, quickly, quickly. Through the moonlight, slowly.

Shadow, quick.

Moonlight, slow.

The dark pit at the corridor's end was a footstep away.

'Duff!' Her voice quavered into the darkness. Somewhere behind her, a snicker spluttered and echoed off the corridor walls. Out of the corner of her eye, something moved on the windowpane. She stayed stock still. She couldn't breathe. She didn't dare look back. Duff had to be nearby, he had to be just a few steps in front of her, but she couldn't make herself go into that blackness. Her palms were clammy, her knees were shaking.

Enough, Jessie Minahan! Enough, already! Don't just stand here like a dummy! Do something! Even inside her head, her voice quavered.

Another snicker, almost at her ear. She swung around.

'Who's there?' she demanded, her voice high but firm. Nothing. She turned to the window. Roofs and moon. She peered back into the blackness where Duff had disappeared.

You can do this, she thought. Just a few steps and you'll have Duff. He has to be there. He has to.

'Cheese and onion?' a mocking voice asked, just behind her.

Jessie turned slowly. 'You!'

'Who'd you think it was, you looper?' G materialised in the shadows, grinning from ear to ear. 'You should have seen yourself, creeping down the corridor like something was going to jump out and murder you any minute. "Duff!"' he mock-sobbed. '"Du-huff! I nee-hed you! Duff, boo-hoo!"'

'But, the window?' Jessie snapped, half angry, half confused. 'That was you? I could have sworn it was—'

'So, are they?' G was staring at her hand.

'What?'

'Are they cheese and onion?' He pointed at the scrunched up packet in her right hand. The crisp bag. She must have been clutching it all the way down the corridor.

'Yes, as it happens,' she said. 'Though I don't see what that has to do with anything.'

'They're my favourites.' G's face was so mournful that Jessie nearly laughed.

G looked around. 'Where is Duffer-dog?'

'There.' Jessie indicated the shadows. 'At least, that's where he has to be. He won't come when I call him.'

'And you're too afraid to go get him?'

Jessie set her mouth in a grim line and stepped towards the darkness.

'Oh, don't be silly. I'll go,' G said. 'Ghostboy saves the day. Again.' He vanished into the black and the corridor fell silent.

Jessie waited. A full minute.

Is he messing? Stop messing! Or is it a trick? What if G and Sully—

A laugh, and the corridor's end lit up to show G floating there. Beneath him on the ground Duff was holding his ratting position: back to the corridor, nose to the wall. Jessie could have cried with relief.

'What's up with him?' G asked, raising his eyebrows

at her. 'He's acting weird. Has he lost it or what?'

'He must have seen the rat again. There was one in the detective office earlier. To Duff, rats are the enemy.'

'Give him a crisp then. If I can't have one, at least share them with Duff, you meaner. I don't know which of you is a bigger weirdo, you, having a party on your own in the middle of the night, or yer dog, staring at the wall like he's only got two brain cells to rub together.'

Jessie tossed some crisps on the floor. Duff gave up his vigil and padded over to eat them.

'It's one of the worst bits about being dead,' sighed G, as Duff snaffled up every last bit. 'Not being able to eat.'

'Not being able to eat spinach?' Jessie asked, with a grin. 'Or brussels sprouts?'

'Roast chicken and stuffing!' G said wistfully.

'Boiled cabbage?'

'Coddle! Toffees, chocolate-chip ice cream!' G shouted, turning upside-down and skipping along the ceiling.

'Semolina pudding? Spam?' Jessie laughed.

'Turkey and ham! Sticky toffee pudding! Pepperoni and mushroom pizza! Chips!' yelled the boy, bouncing above her as she walked backwards along the corridor, back through shadows and moonlight, back towards the remains of her midnight feast.

'Snails? Eels? Fish eggs? Poached frogs' legs?' Jessie giggled.

No reply. The boy had gone quite still, floating just above her, feet on the ceiling, his hair hanging down, the wound on his forehead open and dark against his ghost skin. He was staring at something over Jessie's shoulder. She turned.

'Everything all right, Jessie?' George McCabe asked. He gaped at G and the boy gawked back. They couldn't take their eyes off each other.

'Er, yes. I'm fine, George,' Jessie said. 'This is G.'

'This is G,' George repeated. He frowned and turned his head as far as he could to one side to get a better look at the upside-down boy. He frowned again and shook himself slightly, as if trying to shake something loose back into place.

'G, this is George McCabe,' Jessie said. What was up with G? He looked angry, smash-the-place-up furious.

'I was, em, I was just leaving.' George was speaking to Jessie but he couldn't tear his gaze away from the ghost hanging from the ceiling. Like he'd seen G somewhere before and was trying to work out where. 'If you're sure you're okay, Jessie?'

'I'm fine. Absolutely.' Jessie didn't like the look on G's face at all. She grabbed George's arm and walked him to the door. 'You've been working late. You must be tired, you should go.'

She opened the door and half-pushed him outside.

'Night, then.' She shut the door in the man's face. Through the glass in the door she watched him shake his head and walk down the steps. She heard him rattling his keys as he approached the gates. She listened as he opened the little door set into the left gate and stepped out into the night, clanking it shut behind him. When she was sure he was gone she turned back to face G.

'What wrong?' she asked. The boy was the right way up again and just in front of her.

'George McCabe? His name is George McCabe?' G demanded. 'Is he from around here? What age would you say he is?' G began pacing, walking one way and swooshing the other, the same way Greenwood did.

'Twenty-four, twenty-five,' she replied.

'Maybe the age I'd be if I were alive. I knew it! I knew I'd seen his face somewhere before. He's one of my old gang – Rashers McCabe. He ran out on me the day I had my accident. When the old banger tumbled down the scrapheap, he left me to die all alone, the coward! I didn't get a proper look at his face until tonight, not close up, but it's him all right, I know it is.'

'I think he recognised you too,' Jessie said thoughtfully.

'He'll be sorry he ran out on me, he will.' G's face was contorted with rage; his arms were tight by his sides, his fists balled up. 'He'll be sorry he ever set foot back in this building again. I'll haunt him good and proper. You don't run out on friends like that. You don't let friends down. I'll teach him, I will.'

'Oh.' Jessie regarded the boy for a moment, then raised an eyebrow. 'Is that your friendship code? That's how you believe things should be?'

'Yes!' G snapped back at her. 'You stand by your friends and they stand by you. It's about loyalty. And honour.'

'Really?' Jessie said sharply. 'No walking out on them when things don't go your way, no selling them out first chance you get?' She glared at him. What had she been

161

thinking, mucking about with G, when he'd probably betrayed them to Sully Ellz'mede? 'You're a fine one to be talking about loyalty and honour. You don't know the first thing about them!' she said, her anger as much at herself now as at him.

'I–I–I—' G stuttered, confused.

'Your friends have to go by your rules but you get to break them?' Jessie asked. 'And who are your friends now, G? Me, Jason, Nat and Master Greenwood? Or Sullivan Ellz'mede?'

G slumped down in a heap against a wall. He began to pick at his nails.

'Made a mistake,' he muttered.

'I beg your pardon?'

'Made a mistake, didn't I?'

'Excuse me?'

'The crow. It was him, wasn't it? It was Sullivan Ellz'mede all along. But how was I to know that?' G peeked up at Jessie from under his fringe.

'There was no crow, G, and you know it.'

'There was a crow. But it was him, I know that now.'

'A ghost crow?' Jessie frowned uncertainly.

'Nah, a real crow.'

'Sullivan Ellz'mede was the crow?'

'Yes. At the time I was so amazed to be talking to a crow that it never crossed my mind it might be him. Why would it? It was only when I thought about the things it said to me . . . it asked me stuff, asked me about lifting things, about doing a favour for it and, in return, it said, it might be able to give me back my life. It was Sullivan Ellz'mede. Talking about the power source. It had to be.' He hit his hand against the floor in frustration and it went straight through, overbalancing him.

Jessie stared at him. What if he was telling the truth? He seemed to be serious; as if he was genuinely upset by how things had turned out.

'Can I trust you, G for Ghostboy?' she asked. 'Or is this another one of your games?'

He nodded miserably, his fringe hiding his eyes, then shook his head.

He did help me find Duff, Jessie thought.

As if he had read her mind Duff went over to the distressed boy and sat down beside him, so close he was sitting partly inside the ghost boy's leg. It was exactly the way Duff sat with her when she was upset about something. G looked up in surprise.

'D'you see that?' he smiled at Jessie tentatively. 'He likes me, after all.'

'Hmm.' Jessie chewed her lip.

One last chance, she thought. I'll give him one last chance. What else was she going to do with the rest of the night? Sleep?

'Okay. The crow. The whole story, please. Start from the beginning and don't leave anything out.'

✳✳ 27 ✳✳

'How is Sully Ellz'mede able to turn himself into a live crow?' Jessie asked when G finished talking.

'Because that's the gift the Timecatcher gave him?' suggested G. 'Greenwood got the power to control other ghosts, Blot can pass on pictures from her head, Sully Ellz'mede can turn into a crow. And as a crow, Sully would be able to fly inside the 'catcher.'

'But he can already fly in there as a ghost.' Jessie frowned. 'It doesn't make sense.'

'He can do things as a crow that he can't do as a ghost, but.'

'He can't lift the Ring of Tomar as a crow, it's too heavy.'

'And he'd know I couldn't lift it either, so why was he trying to get me to help him?' G began to pace again.

'Unless—' Jessie put her hand up to halt him '—he doesn't actually know what the power source is yet. He got close enough to it to know more or less where it is and what it can do—'

'But he never actually saw it, so he doesn't know it's a big, heavy thing. That's possible.'

'Or—' Jessie jabbed the air with one finger for emphasis '—he *has* seen it, knows how heavy it is, but only intends taking a part of it.'

'What?'

'Maybe there's a stone set into it that he can peck out as a crow, or a bit he can break off. If the ring is as powerful as Greenwood thinks it is, a small piece of it would probably be pretty powerful too. Enough for whatever Sully Ellz'mede wants it for.'

'Life. That must be it. He wants to be alive again,' G said firmly. 'He thinks it can give him back his life. Greenwood was right, the reality TV stuff was just a smokescreen. But where does Narls Cunningham fit in?'

'I don't know but we've got to tell Greenwood. He's expecting a ghost, not a crow,' Jessie said, jumping up from her window seat. 'You have to tell Greenwood. You're the only one that can get to him.'

'He won't listen to me; he thinks I'm a waste of space.'

'Maybe he does,' Jessie said. 'But that doesn't matter!'

'Eh?' G floated to his feet.

'I mean that's not important now,' Jessie explained. 'What's really important is that he knows about the crow. Even if he doesn't believe you, when he sees the crow he'll be on guard. You've got to warn him.'

'But how do I find him? We don't know where he is. We don't know if he's found the ring at all.'

'I do. He has.'

'You never said.' G pouted.

'Well, I'm saying now.' She hesitated. 'I wasn't sure I could trust you before, was I?'

'And now?' G sounded hurt and hopeful at the same time.

Jessie looked at him. Everything he'd said made some sort of strange sense. But what if he was lying? It would be the biggest mistake she'd ever made. She paused. Somewhere deep inside her she believed G. Trust your instincts, Dad used to say. Well, she would.

'I trust you,' she answered.

G smiled.

'Hey,' he said suddenly. 'What's up with Duff?'

Duff was perched in the window where Jessie had been sitting. He was staring out through the glass and quivering.

'What's he looking at?' G asked, floating into the window ledge behind him.

'I don't know.' Jessie gazed out. Over the roofs of the mill the sky was turning orange and pink. 'Dawn! It's dawn on the longest day.'

They watched for a few moments, watched the darkness give way, watched the sky get brighter and bluer.

'But he's in his rat-alert pose,' G protested. 'Something's bothering him. What is it, Duffer?' He leaned down beside the dog to look out from his angle.

Jessie squinted. 'The sky. It's as if bits of it are shifting around, but that's only the glass. Isn't it?'

They looked at each other in alarm. Duff whined anxiously at their feet.

'Outside, quick!' Jessie jumped off the ledge and ran, Duff at her heels, through the door and out onto the landing of the front stairs. G took a shortcut through the wall and got there before them. They stared at the sky.

Patches of it were moving towards them, rippling. There was a swooshing noise, strangely familiar. Swooshing and babbling, coming closer, like a huge flock of birds, chattering and chittering. It wasn't loud so much as intense, as if it was hitting some unused frequency inside Jessie's head. She put her hands up to her ears. It wasn't all coming from the north, either. The boy and girl turned on the platform, gazing at the four corners of the sky. All was moving, humming with supernatural sound. Jessie shrank down and threw her arms around Duff. G rose several feet off the landing, his face glowing.

'Ghosts!' he said, in an awed voice. 'Hundreds of them! Thousands!'

As he said it, the first group reached the mill and circled, searching, then swooped down, through the Detective Agency's windows.

'It's another diversion!' G gasped. 'That Sully's a clever one, you have to give him that!'

'A diversion? What do you mean?' Jessie could hardly think straight with the noise reverberating in her head. Spirits swept in from all directions.

'D'you remember when Greenwood said none of the ghosts in Dublin would talk to him the other night? Said they were all acting strange? I'll bet this is why.' G ducked as a woman in a large crinoline skirt flew too close. 'Sully's only gone and told them about the Timecatcher, hasn't he? Told them they could have a good old time visiting the past, so here they all are, day-tripping. And I'll bet he told them it didn't open till this morning so they'd all turn up at once.'

Jessie was dismayed. 'It'll be crazy in there. Greenwood is going to have an awful time; he'll be sensing ghosts all over. It'll be mayhem.'

'Yeah! It's really clever.' G smirked.

Jessie looked up at him furiously.

'Oh, it's bad for us, I know.' He tried to look concerned. 'But you have to admit it's clever.'

'It's clever all right. Now you get in there, G, and tell Greenwood what we know and I'll tell Nat and Jason.' Jessie stood up with Duff in her arms.

Through the windows they could see the detectives, leaping around the office, frantically flapping their hands around in the air as if fending off bats.

'What if they won't believe you?' G said, raising his voice above the din. 'What if no one will listen to us?'

'We have to make them,' Jessie shouted. She shifted Duff into one arm and held out her hand.

G looked at it, Jessie's hand stretching towards him. He reached out his own ghost hand and their fingers touched.

'Good luck, G,' Jessie said.

'You too,' he mumbled from under his fringe.

More and more ghosts were flying in. Men, women, children. Every century's dearly departed, every era's thug and thief. So many were arriving now, they were jostling each other on the approach and Jessie could only imagine the crush and queue at the portal. G floated beside her, transfixed.

'What are you waiting for?' she yelled at the boy. 'The future of Dublin could depend on this! Go!'

He shook himself slightly. Jessie was right. This was

168

exactly what he wanted. A task. An adventure. What *was* he waiting for?

It's overwhelming him. He feels a draw, a desire to be part of this, to fly with his own kind. It's like the time his Uncle Bernie brought him to a football match in Croker. The crowd had broken into round after round of Mexican waves. It was brilliant, like being part of some big, jolly, noisy, sweaty monster. He has that same feeling now; excitement thrills through him at the thought of the adventures that may lie just beyond the portal wall. But he also feels suddenly sick. Nerves? Maybe.

He looks back at Jessie; she seems very far away. She's yelling at him again. He can't hear her any more, but he can see her mouth form the words, 'Go, go.'

He watches the incoming waves of spectres flow over the mill roofs from all sides. Unconsciously, he moves his head back and forth as if he's calculating the turn of a skipping rope, waiting for the right moment to run in.

A group of old codgers in business suits. No.

A knot of nuns, black habits flapping. Nooo.

A gang of raggedy boys, a wee band of three. That's more like it. G punches the air with his fist. Yes!

✳✳ 28 ✳✳

$\mathcal{F}$alling. Falling through time and space. Spinning out of control. G heard his own voice screaming.

'Don't fight it,' yelled someone near his ear. A face flashed by, grinning. 'Just let it take you in, that's what the man said! Yahoo!' And the grinner spun away, tumbling and twisting in the current of the Timecatcher.

G took a deep breath, uncurled his arms from his body and spread them out like the grinning boy's. 'Yahoo,' he called shakily.

He had followed the raggedy boys straight through the portal into the Timecatcher. The vortex grabbed hold of them immediately, towing them into its whirling mass and spinning them inwards, downwards. For G, the fall seemed to last forever. He waited for the crash-landing, knowing it was coming, knowing it couldn't hurt him, but the impulse to curl up in a ball to protect himself was almost impossible to resist. Then, just as suddenly as it had snatched them up, the vortex released them and G found himself rolling harmlessly down four stone steps onto a wooden floor, fetching up beside three laughing boys.

'Where are we?' asked the smallest one, a lad in grey knee-length shorts and an oversized shirt.

'It's the detectives' rooms in the mill,' G said, floating

170

to his feet. 'But . . . it's different.' There were no buttons, no machines, no computers. Instead there were old oak desks with inkwells and ledgers spread across them and shelves running floor to ceiling, filled with large books, leatherbound in various shades of darkness, gathering dust.

'I wonder what year it is,' said the tumbler who had grinned at G as they fell. 'I'm Danny, by the way. 1951 to 1964. Knocked off me bike by a scooter in Fishamble street.'

'Hugh,' said the small boy, nodding at G. '1917 to 1928. TB, St James's Hospital.'

'Miles,' said the third boy, trying to dust off his velvet knee breeches which were covered in clay and muck. He was wearing a poncy white shirt with frills at the neck and wrists. G was tempted to sneer but a big gash on one shirt sleeve and a huge red stain at the waist made him hesitate. '1847 to 1860,' continued the boy. 'Murdered by pickpockets in St Stephen's Green.' He lifted the shirt to show a deep knife wound under his left ribs.

'Murdered! Wow, cool!' G nodded appreciatively.

'You?' prompted Danny.

'Oh, right. G,' said G. 'G for Ghostboy. Died, er, ten or more years ago. Head injury sustained in a fall. Here, in the mill yard.' He scraped his fringe back from his forehead to show his cut. 'Messed up me memory a bit.'

'You died in the mill?' Danny looked impressed. 'You know about this Timecatcher-thingy then?'

'Well, yeah, a little,' G said. 'I've never been inside it

before, but,' he added quickly, just in case they expected too much of him.

'So, where are the people? The Sully guy said there'd be shadow people.' Danny went to the window and scanned the yard. All was quiet.

'Well, it's dawn in the real world and all the ghostdays are synchronised with real-time, so if it's five in the morning out there, it's five in the morning in here. Everyone's still asleep.' G grinned, pleased to be able to show off a bit of insider knowledge. Greenwood had explained the time bit to him, though he hadn't used the words 'synchronised' or 'real-time' – G added them for effect. The 'catcher seemed to demand a little sophistication.

'What time did the rebellion start?' Danny turned to Hugh. 'Are we too early or should we head there now?'

'It didn't start till noon,' said Hugh.

'What rebellion? What are you talking about?' G asked.

'Easter Rising, Monday, 24th April 1916 to be exact,' Danny replied. 'We've all picked something we want to go see. I picked the Beatles concert at the Adelphi in 1963. Me ma wouldn't let me go, said I was too young. That gets put right tonight, yeah, yeah, yeah!' He mimed playing a guitar, swinging his head wildly to make his dead short hair wobble about a bit.

'I have chosen the first recital of Handel's Messiah in 1742,' Miles announced, placing left fingertips to right fingertips and considering G over the top of the resulting steeple. 'Care to join me?'

Danny and Hugh cracked up at G's alarmed expression.

'Nope! He'll be coming to the Beatles with me and Hugh. That's right, isn't it, G, boyo?' Danny said, when he had stopped laughing and let go of his ribcage.

'Sure,' said G. And maybe he could go with them, too. After he delivered his message to Greenwood maybe there'd be time to join this gang of lads and have some fun.

'That's my choice. But Hugh's choice is best of all,' Danny was saying.

Hugh glowed with pleasure. 'I chose the Easter Rising,' he said. 'Real, live battles right in O'Connell Street. There'll be guns and explosions and soldiers and rebels. Me da used to tell me about it, he did.'

'Cool,' said G.

Danny nodded agreement. 'But what'll we do until then?'

'The zoo,' said G wistfully. 'Let's go to the zoo.' He should go find Greenwood right away, he knew he should. But the zoo. He'd really love to go see the zoo again. It wasn't far from Manor Street; his gran used to bring him.

Miles looked puzzled. 'We don't need the Timecatcher to visit the zoo, old chap. We can go there any time!'

'Oh, right.' G pulled a face. 'You can; I can't. I can't go outside the mill at all.'

The three raggedy boys looked appalled.

'And will it be the same in here, amongst the shadow days?' asked Miles.

G could feel his ghost heart drop down to his runners. He hadn't thought of that.

'Let's find out,' suggested Danny, and flew out into the yard.

G followed slowly. The mill looked much the same as always. A stone cage for a boy to spend forever in. He crossed his fingers and floated upwards, cautiously. In real time, he couldn't fly any higher than the highest roofline. He inched higher, higher.

Yes!

He began to fly in earnest, upwards to get his first view of the city in years. Rows and rows of chimneys running north; the river glittering to the south. He zigzagged above the mill, happily overshooting the walls.

'Go, G, go!' chanted the three boys below him.

He rejoined them, grinning from ear to ear.

'The zoo it is,' said Miles. 'Only let's make it 1855.'

'Why?' chimed G and the other two.

'That's when it got the first pair of lions,' Miles said, with a lofty smile. 'Now, how do we get out of here and back to the beginning of this thing?'

They all turned to G expectantly.

'Eh ...' G racked his brain for more of the bits Greenwood had told him. 'We all start at the same spot where we dropped in – the four steps – and, em, fly upwards till the 'catcher grabs us again.'

'You first, then,' said Danny, pointing back to the office windows. 'We'll be right behind you.'

Just the zoo, I'll just go to the zoo, thought G, as he passed back through the glass and flew towards the top of the four steps.

In his mind's eye he could see Jessie. 'Go, go,' she was shouting. She'd be mad at him for visiting the zoo, but he'd been cooped up inside the mill so long. He couldn't stay here another minute.

And Greenwood probably won't listen to a word I say, anyway, he thought. So another hour won't make any difference.

He went through the bricks into the void beyond. He was feeling a little odd, like he was in a car going too fast on a bumpy road. What was it he was supposed to tell old Greenwood anyway? Something about Sully what's-his-face? For a moment G tried hard to remember. Then the Timecatcher had him in its grip again and he was shooting upwards. He spread his arms out like a bird.

'Yahoo!' he yelled.

'Yahoo!' Three answering calls rose up from below him.

29

'For heaven's sake, Jessie, you can't be serious!' Jason shouted to make himself heard over the whine of incoming ghosts. He and Nat were lying flat on the office floor, watching the portal. Jessie had dropped down beside them as soon as she let herself in through the door and Duff was half underneath her, his nose tucked into his paws. Ghosts were skimming above their heads from every angle. Jessie was trying to tell Jason and Nat about the crow but somehow it was coming out wrong. Having to yell wasn't helping.

'But G said the crow—'

'I think we've established that what G says can't be taken seriously,' Jason snapped. He ducked his head as a fat man swooped over him, his stomach brushing through Jason's hair.

'But the crow isn't a crow—'

'Because there never was a crow in the first place. We know that already.' Jason threw her a look of pure exasperation. 'Look at what's happening here, Jessie! It's a disaster! We've got to keep track of the numbers of ghosts entering the Timecatcher.' He scribbled some marks on a crumpled paper bag which was on the floor just under his chin. Nat was using buttons as counters, furiously adding to a pile in front of her as new ghosts swept over, her eyes darting around the room.

The portal was wide open and a constant blur of flying spectres was shooting through it into the Timecatcher. There were too many of them coming at the portal too fast; some were failing to gain entry at their first attempt and bouncing off the surrounding bricks. They floated for a moment in stunned surprise before trying again or immediately lapped the room and rejoined the flow. The noise in the office was horrible, a mixture of full-volume dentist's drill and a hundred crying cats.

'But the crow is Sully,' Jessie yelled desperately. 'Please, Jason. You've got to listen to me,'

'Not now, Jessie.' He jotted more marks on the paper bag.

She was just about to tell him that Greenwood had found the ring then realised that at least a hundred passing ghosts would hear her too. This was hopeless. She had to at least give Jason Greenwood's message. She snatched the paper bag and pencil from Jason's hands.

'Greenwood has found ring,' she wrote. 'Sully is crow.' Jason looked at it for a moment then crawled across the floor to his desk. He reached his hand up and slid his laptop off. He passed it to Jessie and grabbed her bag and pushed that towards her too. He mimed typing.

'Write it down,' he yelled. 'We'll read what you have to say when this slows.' He pointed towards the back room. 'Do it in there, it's got to be quieter. Stay in there until it's time for school, Jessie, okay?' She nodded and, hugging the laptop to her, got to her feet. 'And don't come back here again today, Jess. I must have been crazy to let you stay last night. It's too dangerous. Stay away, understand?'

He looked at her to check she had heard him. She nodded again and dashed over to the back-room door, keeping her head low, Duff sticking close to her ankles.

She stumbled into the other room, slammed the door and leaned against it, shaking the shivery feel of ghosts from her hair. She pulled a ratty fur coat from a hanger, tugged it around her shoulders and sat down on a pile of old clothes. Everything was going wrong. Sullivan Ellz'mede had outmanoeuvred them and reduced their plans to chaos. He must have been in the mill all along, listening to them. Jessie shuddered and Duff licked her face. Now, to make matters worse, she suddenly realised she'd never actually told G which day Greenwood was in.

'Where are you, G?' she cried. 'Try and find Greenwood, please, G. You've got to try.' The whine of ghosts over the mill drowned her voice.

She opened the laptop and began to type. First her conversation with Master Greenwood, then G's story of meeting the crow. She tried to report everything word for word. She clicked save just as it turned eight o' clock. More than three hours since dawn, since all the ghosts had turned up, since G had entered the Timecatcher. She listened for a moment. No ghost noise. Everything was quiet. She pulled on her school uniform and opened the door to the front office. Jason and Nat were asleep on the floor. They were still in their counting positions, Nat unconscious on her button pile and Jason dribbling onto the paper bag.

They've hardly slept for two nights in a row, Jessie thought, stifling a yawn herself. I'll just leave this here where they can see it when they wake up.

She put the laptop back on Jason's desk and left it open with her report on the screen. The low battery sign was flashing so she found the flex and plugged it into a nearby socket.

'Okay. I've done everything I can. Time to get you home, Duffer-dog. We'll need to run if I'm going to make school on time.'

✳✴ 30 ✴✳

$\mathcal{F}$iguring out the Timecatcher took a while. At first G and the raggedy boys couldn't stop themselves being pulled in every time they reached the beginning, so they kept landing in random days. It was Miles who worked out that if they floated side-on to the flow of the vortex they could hold their position at the edge of its slipstream, just inside the entrance portal.

Now that he could watch it whirl by, G saw wave upon wave of folds and openings within it. Hundreds of ghosts were diving and surfacing all around him and he remembered something else Greenwood had told him about the 'catcher.

'Shout out the date you want to visit,' G shouted to Miles. 'And it will come to us.'

Soon. He'd go find Greenwood soon. When he got back from the zoo.

'26th August, 1855,' yelled Miles.

The Timecatcher swirled and slowed and one of the waves yawned wider right in front of them. Easy peasy. Too easy; why was it so easy? But G didn't really care.

He turned to face the opening. 'Go!' he yelled, and was immediately sucked in.

'Go, go, go,' yelled the raggedy boys.

The zoo was cool. Small, much smaller than when he and Gran had visited last, but deadly all the same. Most of the animals were just waking up and he and the boys were able to float into the cages, up close. The boys saw their first shadow people, keepers starting their working day, feeding and cleaning out.

It was fun but odd at the same time, like falling inside a telly. Nobody reacted to G and the raggedy boys because nobody was really there. It didn't matter, though, because they were four, four boys out to have some craic. Deadly.

All the while a little voice kept nagging in the back of G's head, 'You're not supposed to be here. You have a job to do.' But G ignored it. He was having fun.

Miles kept announcing bird and animal facts, G and Danny made poo jokes and Hugh invented a game where whoever was 'it' made an animal noise and last one in the correct cage was out. They played for ages; they played until the sun was shining directly above their heads.

The Rebellion, on the other hand, was a real downer. They tried to act like this was a game too, but their laughter sounded hollow against the screams of the wounded men and the gunfire. Shells were exploding inside and outside the rebels' headquarters. The noise was awful; G would never forget it.

A boy was slumped in a corner, behind a pillar; he was probably only a few years older than G. Tears were rolling down his face and he was whimpering for his ma. He clutched his tummy like he had a bellyache.

'He's scared, I guess,' said Danny.

'I think I would be, too.' Hugh hunkered down and reached out as if to touch the boy's hand.

'Still—' G pulled a face '—I'd like to think I'd be out there fighting, not back here hiding.'

Danny and Miles nodded, Hugh said nothing. The shadowboy went on crying. Suddenly he looked up, stared hard over their shoulders and gave a gurgling cough. His eyes went blank. His hand fell away from his belly. His belly had a hole in it.

No one said anything. They all took to the air and floated quickly back to Stoneybatter. When they were in the mill, on the steps, ready to use the exit portal, Miles stopped.

'Time's getting on,' he said. 'I think it's time to split up for a bit, do our home visits.'

'Eh?' G blinked. 'Home visits?'

'Yes, of course. All want to drop in and see our maters and paters, don't we?' Miles raised his eyebrows at G.

'Our mas and das,' translated Danny, rolling his eyes. 'They should be up and about now. I'm going to do me last Christmas, when I got me bike. That was a good day.'

'I'm going to do my seventh birthday,' said Hugh. 'Me da made me a hobby horse from a broom handle and we had bread and butter pudding.'

'I'm going to visit my own funeral,' announced Miles. 'I am very curious to see what it was like. And you, G? Have you no home to go to?'

'Of course I do!' G snapped.

Miles began to raise his eyebrows again, then seemed

to think better of it. G could feel himself glaring. The raggedy boys were looking at him funny.

'What are you staring at?' The words hovered on the tip of his tongue but he bit them back. The boys' faces swam in front of him and blurred. He could see Jessie again, she was shouting at him, shouting, 'Go'. Go where? He couldn't remember.

'Sorry,' said G to the waiting boys. 'It's just I have something else I'm supposed to do. I think.'

'What do you mean?' asked Danny. They all looked at G curiously.

'Oh, nothing. Doesn't matter.' He could see they were dying to ask more questions but he wasn't sure he could answer them. He was feeling queasy again. He had come into the Timecatcher for a reason, something important. To find Greenwood, that was it. But why? He searched his memory. Blurs and blanks. He shook his head and his stomach reeled.

The raggedy boys were still staring.

'Me gran,' G said. 'I'll go and see me gran.'

They split up when they reached the entrance portal. G promised Danny and Hugh he'd meet them at the Beatles concert later on, then let them all dive into the Timecatcher ahead of him. He hovered on its edge for a few minutes.

'Greenwood. Gran. Greenwood. Gran.' He felt like his head would explode. 'Greenwood or Gran? Well, that's a no-brainer, isn't it?'

Which year to choose? Fourteen years ago, just to be sure he was still alive. And right in the middle of the summer, so as it wouldn't be a school day.

He didn't even look out through the windows into the yard when he got there; he didn't want to see the old scrapheap. He flew up through the roof and over the stables next door, into Manor Street. There was the post office and the sweetshop where he used to get his favourite crisps. Walsh's pub on the corner and the barbershop where he and Gran would fight about how short a cut he was going to get this time.

Wish Jessie was here, he thought. Like her to see me gran.

And there was Gran's house.

Home.

He hesitated at the door. The window was open; he could hear her voice.

'You be back here by teatime, do you hear me? And no messing around in that old mill yard. I've told you before it's not safe. Owner should have fixed that lock by now, I told him it was broke. Didn't tell him it was you what broke it, though!'

'I never did!' His own voice floated out the window towards him.

'Don't tell fibs, G. You think I don't know what you and your pals get up to?'

G. She called him G. So he hadn't forgotten what he was called when he was alive. It was obviously short for something other than Ghostboy. A real name. His real name. What, but?

Oh, please don't let it be Gavin, he thought, scrunching up his face at the thought. Or Graham. Or Gerald.

He floated upwards so he could see her, his gran. A helmet of brown waves petrified into place with hairspray which, he remembered, always smelt of roses. Glasses so big they nearly covered her face. She was giving out to the boy at the table but there was a twinkle in her eye. The boy was cheeky-faced, tanned, uncombed. He sparkled and fizzed like freshly shaken lemonade.

'Off with you now, you scamp,' she said, and the boy was up and running to the door.

'See ya, Gran,' he called back over his shoulder, then he was out on the street, galloping past G. Gran came out to close the door, taking a moment to look up the road after her grandson. G wanted to watch her a little longer but the need to follow that shadow of himself tugged at him.

'See ya, Gran,' he whispered and he floated after the running boy.

He knew where the shadow G was going. To the mill, of course. That's where they'd gone every day, him and the gang. He watched his shadow reach the gates, wiggle the broken lock off and tug open the bolt of the little door. If the bolt wasn't open yet that meant he was the first of the gang to get there, which meant he could bag the Morris Minor. It was the best thing in the scrapyard and whoever got there first claimed it for the day. The shadow G whooped in delight and scrambled in the door, clambering past some bags and bins and pipes blocking the archway.

G waited at the doorway for a second before following himself in. It's just like that day, he thought. The day of the accident. He felt cold. Which was odd, him being a ghost.

G watched the boy begin to clamber up the scrapheap towards his prize. The car was so high up it was level with the first-storey windows. The climbing boy was laughing and humming to himself as he went.

'I'm the king of the castle, get DOWN you dirty rascal.'

G began to shiver.

'Whoa!' Something in the scrapheap shifted and the shadowboy grabbed onto a protruding metal bar as one foot slid suddenly into midair. He swung precariously for a moment then steadied himself.

That was a near one! G thought.

'That was a near one,' said the scrapheap scaler with a shaky laugh.

Memories crashed into place inside G's head.

'This is it,' he said aloud. 'This is the day I died.'

He thought he had chosen a random day to visit his gran, but he hadn't. He'd chosen his last day alive, in his last summer as a live boy.

I just wanted to visit any old day, he thought. Not this one. What made me pick this day? I've come to watch myself die. Just for a second he wondered if the 'catcher was playing games with him. Nah, couldn't be. It was just a rotten coincidence.

He was feeling queasy again. Everything was reeling around and he wished he could lean against a wall to steady himself. He focused on the climbing boy. His old self was nearly at the car, he was reaching for the open driver's door and pulling himself in. He slammed the door and the pile shifted slightly. He laughed and turned the steering wheel. Under the car the wheels turned left then right and the heap shifted again.

G closed his eyes. He couldn't watch. The boy had only minutes to live and he was laughing. Any second the others would arrive, Rashers McCabe and Snotzer and Spud. Then the heap would shudder and the Morris Minor would begin to tumble. Make it stop. Somebody, make it stop.

He wished he could yell out a warning, but that was just stupid. The boy wasn't really there.

G opened his eyes again. He blinked. There was someone in the office windows, a faint figure watching the boy from the other side of the yard. G floated up, closer.

Greenwood!

A shadow of Greenwood, back then, on that day, watching him in the car, scowling at him. G flew right up to the window and stuck out his tongue right in the enemy's face. The shadow Greenwood didn't react, just continued to glare at the boy in the teetering car.

'Did you watch me die, you old looney man?' G roared at the shadow. 'You did, didn't you? You could have stopped it but you just stood there and let it happen. Well, two can play at that game!'

He didn't look back. He heard the door in the gate open as the other boys arrived, he heard himself shouting hello from the car, he heard that ominous creaking, but he didn't turn. He shot through the wall in search of the portal. He was back inside the Timecatcher in seconds. He whirled upwards to the edge of the vortex.

'5th July, 1201,' he yelled at the swirling mass of days.

The Timecatcher slowed. An opening yawned beside him. G turned and it sucked him in.

✶✶ 31 ✶✶

Miss O'Dea phoned Mrs Minahan straight after lunch and suggested she come and collect Jessie from school early.

'She's looking peaky, very peaky, Mrs Minahan. I think she should be home in bed.' Miss O'Dea tipped Jessie's chin up with her hand and tut-tutted at the paleness of her skin. 'Five minutes? See you then, Mrs Minahan.'

Miss O'Dea smiled kindly at Jessie and told her to pack up her schoolbag. Shoving books and copies into her backpack gave Jessie a chance to sneak a look at her mobile. She'd been hoping the detectives would let her know what they thought about her report on the crow. But there was nothing from Nat.

Jessie propped her head up in one hand and her eyelids began to droop. She'd try Nat's mobile again when she got home, see what they had to say. Something was tap-tapping at the window. She opened her eyes. Moonlight was streaming into the mill corridor. A crow was glaring in at her through the glass. Heavy thuds rained down on the roof above her head, making her jump. More crows, more glittering eyes watching her, daring her to come out into the yard. Crows everywhere, everything turning black.

189

'Jessie, your mam's here.' Miss O'Dea shook her awake. Mrs Minahan was outside, tapping on the class window with her keys, smiling in at Jessie anxiously. The girls nearest were waving out at Duff and cooing.

'I'll go and meet her.' Jessie stood up quickly and grabbed her bag.

'So which one is Geena?' Mam asked when Jessie got outside. The whole class was watching and Mam waved. Jessie steered her towards the gate.

'She went home this morning, never came in to school at all.'

'You girls didn't sleep last night, did you?'

'Not much.' Jessie shrugged.

'Don't worry, I didn't tell your teacher you'd been having a sleepover on a week night.' Mam smiled. 'She'd have told me off for letting you, even if it was in aid of homework.'

'Right.' Jessie smiled weakly and yawned.

'Bed?' suggested Mam. 'Duff's been snoring all day. How about a hot chocolate, bed, and I'll wake you up at teatime?'

'Sounds good.' Jessie linked her arm through her mam's and leaned her head against her as they walked. Duff trotted ahead of them, sniffing.

'Did you get your bag of treats?' her mam asked. 'That George is a nice guy. Odd, but nice.'

'Mmm.'

'But I suppose that's because of his accident.'

'Accident?'

'He nearly died in an accident when he was a kid.

He did die, technically; they revived him in the ambulance on the way to hospital. We'd better get some milk for that hot chocolate.' Mam turned in the door of Maureen's Newsagents.

'It happened in the mill,' Mam continued, rummaging in her wallet for change.

'What did?' Jessie asked absently, flicking through a comic in the magazine stand.

'George's accident. There used to be a scrapheap in the yard, apparently. He was playing in an old car and it turned over. Split open his forehead. He still has the scar.' Mrs Minahan picked up the carton of milk and walked out of the shop. Jessie shoved the comic back into the rack and dashed out after her. She ran in front of her mother, forcing her to a stop.

'Did you say George actually died?' she asked urgently.

'Yes, for three whole minutes. Imagine!' Mam shook her head at the thought of it. 'He says he lost practically all memory of his childhood. Isn't that sad? But I suppose he's lucky to be alive.' She frowned at Jessie. 'What is it, Jess? You look like you've seen a ghost!'

Jessie shook her head. 'It's nothing,' she said, though her heart was beating so fast she could hardly breathe.

Her mam walked on. 'And the strangest thing happened while George was telling me about his accident. We saw a rat, right in the middle of the floor. Watching us.'

'A rat?' Jessie said, a few steps behind.

'In George's studio. I know this sounds nuts but the thing actually began to dance.'

'Dance?' Jessie tried to keep her voice calm.

'Yes. Even did a couple of cartwheels.'

'Really?' Jessie smiled weakly. 'A dancing rat, imagine. Must have been someone's pet, a trained rat.'

'But it was a regular brown one, that's the thing. And it kept gibbering at us, like it was talking. Horrible creature.' Mrs Minahan shuddered.

'Mam?' Jessie bit her lip.

Mrs Minahan turned to look at her.

'I'm sorry, Mam, but I really have to go to the mill. It's important.'

'But we're nearly home! No, Jess. You're exhausted. You spend way too much time there as it is.' Mrs Minahan's face set determinedly.

Jessie took a deep breath. 'Please. Someone else needs to know what you just told me, about G-George.'

Her mother looked at her for a moment. 'You used to tell *me* stuff, Jessie. Now you're all secrets and I don't know what to think.'

Jessie blushed. 'Please, Mam. Trust me?' she asked quietly.

She could see the anxiety on her mam's face. She could see her mam struggling to control it.

Mrs Minahan sighed. 'Okay, okay. But you have to come home at six for tea. Right?'

'Right.' Jessie gave her a quick hug. 'Thanks, Mam. See ya.'

Jessie turned and ran back onto Manor Street, Duff at her heels. She looked at her watch. It was a quarter to two. She couldn't quite take in all the implications of what she'd just heard. But she knew she had to do something, tell someone, before something bad happened. Time was running out. She hoped she wasn't too late.

✳✳ 32 ✳✳

*D*ark.

Not the mill, then, G thought, as he lit himself up to see his surroundings. The tree. Of course! I'm inside the hollow oak tree.

He floated up into the tree's branches, then higher into a bright blue sky. He looked about. Below him was a grove of oaks and to his left, a river. With a start he realised it must be the Liffey. On the other side of the river there was a high wall and inside it a castle, some churches and hundreds of ramshackle houses tumbled about.

'Dublinia, I presume,' he said to himself.

He looked the other way and saw a village sprawling into farmland and forest. Old Stoneybatter. He could hear birds and the rustle of a thousand leaves, the occasional mooing of cows. A dog barking. And something else. In the distance, the sound of many voices. He floated higher and just at the edge of his vision, to the west of the trees, he saw a clearing full of people. He was about to fly towards it when voices close by caught his attention.

'What's goin' on?' a man's voice asked.

'You a stranger here?' The owner of the female voice didn't wait for a reply. 'Sure and everyone that's anybody knows today is a hangin' day at Gibbet's Glade.'

'And a fine day for it, too.' Another female voice. 'Always a shame when it rains at a hangin', puts a real damper on things, so it does.'

The man gave a non-committal grunt. 'I was after a spot o' grub, meself. Is there a local inn does a decent pie and ale?'

'If it's pies you're after there'll be a stand at the hangin',' the first woman said.

G floated over the treetops to look at the three prattlers. The man was smiling broadly.

'Pie and a hangin'! I've never been to one before,' he said cheerily. 'Sure that's grand.'

'Never been to a hangin'?' exclaimed the first woman. She was large and round and when she spoke her mouth showed more gaps than teeth. 'You're in for a treat, you are!'

'Aye,' said the second woman.

'A half dozen to hang and one of them is a famous outlaw,' continued the first woman. 'Beginner's luck, that's what you've got.'

'Famous outlaw?' said the man, as they all began walking.

'Famous in England, they say.' The first woman dropped her voice to a whisper. 'He lived here amongst us for a whole year under a false name and not a soul knowed it was him.'

'Not a soul,' the second woman said.

'Well, we best get a move on, or we'll miss it,' said the first woman. 'We're late. We've certainly missed all the best spots and it's quite possible all the pies will be gone by now, too. So it is.'

G didn't wait to hear the man's response to that. He flew up and over the trees. How could Greenwood just have let die him in the mill yard all those years ago? G blinked back angry tears. His old enemy was about to hang here in this shadowland and G wasn't going to miss it listening to three old codgers waffling in a lane.

✳✳ 33 ✳✳

The queasiness was getting worse. G retched a couple of times watching the first group of men and women hang. Around him some people were stuffing their faces with pies or bread and cheese and guzzling big tankards of ale. Nearly everyone seemed to be having a good day out. G watched from the back of the crowd, staying near the trees.

Greenwood was easy to spot, standing in the second batch of condemned, towering between a skinny dark man and a bald man with freckles big as ladybirds. G thought Greenwood looked distracted, as if he was hardly aware that he was about to die. The skinny man was fidgeting and talking beside him. Sully Whatsit? Had to be.

Why are you here? said the little voice inside G's head.

G shook himself. He couldn't concentrate; pictures were wandering around inside his head. His gran. The young rebel clutching his belly. Danny and the raggedy boys. The Morris Minor. Jessie, saying something he couldn't hear. Something important. If only he could remember.

He straightened up and floated closer to the gallows. I'm here to watch Greenwood die, that's it, he thought. He watched me die, so I'll watch him hang. Seems fair enough.

You're being spiteful. Nasty. The little voice, again.

'Shut up, you. You're nothing but a spoilsport!' G snapped.

But the little voice wouldn't shut up. *You have something important to do,* it said, *and you're wasting time. Go!*

G frowned. The little voice sounded a lot like Jessie.

'Focus, Ghostboy!' he growled to himself. 'Greenwood is the enemy. Greenwood is the enemy. Greenwood is the enemy.'

The bald man was dead, swinging. Greenwood was next. The crowd suddenly went quiet. The man overseeing the hangings frowned and his dark eyes narrowed under the shadow of his floppy hat. He turned in his chair and nodded at the town crier, who was announcing each condemned man and his crimes. Up until this moment he had been doing so to roars of approval.

'This man has been found guilty of multiple crimes of theft, too many to recite here or we'd have to hold over hangin' him till tomorrow!' This line usually got a laugh, but not today.

'He only stole from those what have too much already.' A voice rose up from the depths of the throng. 'That's what I heard.'

There was a general murmuring and many heads across the field nodded in agreement.

'And I heard he did give away most of what he stole, any road!' Another hidden know-it-all.

The man in the hat looked furious.

'Get on with it,' he hissed at the crier.

'Yes, my lord justiciar!' The crier bowed.

'This man has been found guilty of treason!' he continued.

'Hooray for treason!' Someone shouted from the middle of a group of tall men right in the front row. They all feigned shock, dropped their jaws in mock-horror then smiled innocently and batted their eyelids at the raging justiciar.

'Speed it up,' he snarled, poking the crier in the ribs with the handle of his sword.

'He is branded a traitor to King John, Lord of Ireland!' quavered the crier quickly.

'Hooray!' cheered the crowd.

'Absconding from justice! Resisting arrest!'

'Hooray!'

'He has been found guilty of all of these crimes and is sentenced to hang by the neck until dead.'

The crowd went quiet again. The crier was sweating now. It drip-dripped off his chin and two dark circles were forming under his armpits.

'The prisoner is known by several names.'

G moved closer. So Master Greenwood is an alias, he thought. What's your real name then, you thief, liar, traitor, you? He hiccupped loudly and covered his mouth quickly with his hand, looking around to see if anyone had heard him.

'Rrargh! They're not really here, you big eejit!' he whispered to himself. 'This isn't real.'

But his confusion was real enough. Greenwood was

his enemy. He wanted him to have feet of clay, to be a bad man. He wanted to see him die. Didn't he?

So why are you crying? whispered that annoying little voice.

Why did he want to make this stop, to urge the crowd to save this man? Why did he need everything the town crier said to be untrue?

He floated right up to the big shade.

'Who are you?' he sobbed. 'What have you done?'

The shadow Greenwood was staring at the trees. Back in the direction of the spelled oak and the Timecatcher.

'He is known as Reynold Greenleaf,' intoned the crier.

'God bless him,' called a voice.

'John Little,' said the crier.

'God bless him,' chorused the crowd.

'John o' the greenwood.'

'God bless him!'

Through his hiccups and sniffs G heard the crier call one more name to which the crowd sighed back 'God bless him, God bless him, God bless him!'

And then they cheered.

Not for Greenwood's death but for his life. The town crier shrank back into the shadows of the gallows, the justiciar looked shaken. He nodded to the hangman who stood on a box in front of Greenwood with the noose ready in his hand.

G didn't stay to see, he couldn't see anyway. Through a blur of tears he raced back over the trees to the old oak. In minutes he was spiralling in the Timecatcher, spat up on its edges, turning sideways to fight its pull.

The real Greenwood had to be in the Timecatcher somewhere. But which day? He didn't know. Now what? He cupped his hands around his mouth.

'John Greenwood,' he yelled into the void. 'Little John of the greenwood.'

✳✴ 34 ✳✴

Jason sat down heavily in his chair and covered his face with his hands.

'Give me a minute, let me take this in,' he said.

Jessie sat down on a stool and waited. Nat leaned against the desk and chewed her nails. She had a stunned expression on her face and kept opening her mouth to start a new question then shaking her head and attacking another fingernail. Duff gave up expecting a biscuit and flopped down in the shade with a sigh.

'Okay.' Jason dragged his fingers down to his chin and pointed out at the yard. 'Let's get this straight: George McCabe died out there in an accident just like G's?'

'Only he was resuscitated on the way to hospital.' Jessie nodded.

'He has the scar like G's,' said Nat.

'And no memories of his childhood,' continued Jessie.

'So George McCabe is – I just can't get my head around this – George McCabe is—'

'G.' Jessie gulped. 'Grown up.'

'And G is?' Nat, confused, waved her hands in the air.

'The ghost of George's childhood?' suggested Jason.

'That would mean that George is one half of G and G is the other half of George.' Nat raised her eyebrows. 'Phew! It is incredible, totally wild.'

'It's even stranger than the crow thing,' said Jessie. 'You've read my report?'

Jason shook his head. 'We couldn't access it. That dratted rat must have chewed through the computer cord, so it never recharged. Nat spotted it this morning, scuttling away.' He held up the two ends of the flex. 'Computer was dead as a log and I suppose we didn't really think the crow thing was important, Jessie.'

Nat raised her eyebrows. 'Crows, rats, this place is like a zoo.'

Something clicked inside Jessie's brain. 'My mam, she saw the rat when she was here. She said it was dancing. A dancing rat and a talking crow, what's going on?'

'Hmm.' Jason frowned. 'You'd better fill us in now. Start with the crow, Jessie.'

★

'So Sullivan Ellz'mede is able to turn into a crow?' Nat shook her head at the craziness of it all. 'And a rat, too?'

'And he wants the power source so he can live again as a man. He told G that he knows how to get new life for himself,' said Jessie.

Jason screwed up his face, considering. 'Maybe a ghost could shape-shift into a spirit crow, but a real live one? No. I think what G saw was a crow whose body had been taken over by Sully.'

'And the rat?' asked Nat.

'Ditto.'

'So how's he going to become a live human being again?' asked Jessie, then gasped, appalled by the answer.

'Oh my God,' said Jason. 'Sully wants the power source so he can *take over* the body of a man.'

'Terribles!' Nat exclaimed. 'And I know who he was planning on taking over!'

'Me!' said a shocked voice behind them.

Duff rose up with a snarl. They all turned to see Narls Cunningham standing in the open doorway. He was blinking and moving his head slowly from side to side like a snake who can't decide who to bite first.

'I knew he could take over the bodies of rats,' he croaked. 'I even kept one for him, fed it, cleaned out its cage.' He shuddered and wiped his hands on his jacket. 'But he said he could only do it with small creatures, docile ones like Ratty-boy – that's what he calls the filthy thing.'

Nat walked over to Narls and looked him in the eye. 'You can confirm that Sullivan Ellz'mede is able to possess a rat and that he has trained one with the intention of using it to enter the Timecatcher. Yez?'

'Yes.' Narls blinked at her in surprise.

'And at what time did he arrange to meet you here today?'

'Three.'

'And what time is it now?'

'Two-thirty.'

'Then I would be leaving, if I were you.'

'But the television shows?' He looked at them hopefully. 'That wasn't a lie? I can still roll out my reality shows?'

Jason, Nat and Jessie shook their heads.

'But it was his dream! He used to tell me that if he could just live out his dreams through me—' Narls Cunningham tailed off with a horrified look on his face '—it would make him a happy man,' he finished in a choked whisper.

'I think he may have meant that literally.' Jason tried to look sympathetic.

Narls began to shake. He was quite a sight, bloodless and rattling inside his sharp black suit. He stumbled backwards out onto the steps and ten seconds later an engine roared to life in the yard and the silver car skidded out under the arch.

'Now what?' Nat asked urgently. 'If Sully manages to steal the source and Narls isn't here when he comes out of the portal, what will he do? Attack one of us?'

'George,' said Jessie, horrified. 'Sully overheard him tell my mam about his accident and that's when he began to dance.'

Nat shuddered. 'That means Sully knows that George only has half a spirit, so wouldn't he think—'

'—that George would make a super-easy target for a bodysnatch? Yes!' Jason raked his hair savagely. 'We've got to get this information to G and Greenwood. But how?'

They all fell silent.

'Blot!' Jessie said suddenly. 'Blot could do it.'

** 35 **

$\mathcal{B}$eneath the tug of the Timecatcher, G felt a more familiar draw, a vacuum cleaner turned fully on him. He shot straight through the trunk of the old oak out into the forest where Greenwood stood glowering, his arms outstretched. He was using his powers to draw G to him and the boy came to an abrupt halt in mid-air, a couple of centimetres from the big ghost's nose.

'What are you wantin' now, Pooka-boy?' Greenwood snarled.

'Are you really Little John? *The* Little John?' G could hear his voice quavering, but he was too excited to take a deep breath.

'I ha' been known as Little John, I own to that name.' Greenwood looked puzzled.

'As in Little John and Robin Hood?' G shouted, wriggling like a hooked fish.

Greenwood crossed his arms and G was free, but he wasn't going anywhere until he had his answer.

'Now where did you get that name from?' The man's eyes narrowed as he considered the boy in front of him. 'What's it to thee if Robin o' the hood was a friend o' mine? What trick are you playin'? Did Sully Ellz'mede put thee up to this?'

'There's no tricks. I've read all your adventures, I know all about you,' G exclaimed.

Greenwood's brow furrowed. 'What are you gabbin' about?'

'You and Robin Hood, you're famous.' Even as G said it he realised how meaningless it sounded.

'Famous, eh? Well, Rob would ha' liked that.' Greenwood shrugged. 'Is that all? Is that what you came to say?'

'No, that's not all,' said G. He glared at the big ghost and tried to control his quivering lip. He bit down hard on it to stop himself shouting his thoughts out loud – I read that book ten times! You were my hero, I wanted to be you. I wanted to be your friend, hang out with you, but that was impossible because you were a character in a book, you were a legend. I'd have climbed into that book if I could have.

And all these years together in the mill they had been enemies; G could have wept with frustration. Instead he spluttered, 'You've been horrible to me! You've been mean! I'm dead and all alone and you never even tried to be k-kind. Fourteen years and you never even gave me a ch-chance.'

Greenwood raised his eyebrows. 'Fourteen years? Could have sworn 'twere only ten. I've lost count o' the centuries, let alone the years ...' He trailed off as he took in the expression on the boy's face. There was real despair mixed with the usual angry defiance and the lad was knuckling his eyes furiously to block tears.

'Rob and the boys seem like a dream I had. Can't even remember half their names now,' Greenwood said, so softly that G barely caught the words. 'I made a mistake when I opened the portal to the Timecatcher, Pooka-boy. 'Twas an accident but 'twas my doin'. I won't leave this earth until I make it right, however long it takes.'

'But you watched me die!' G yelled. 'You could have warned me.'

'I considered warnin' thee! That car waverin' all about and you payin' no heed.' Greenwood shook his head. 'But I was afraid if a ghost appeared in front o' thee, all o' a sudden, it would more likely cause an accident than stop one. I left it to fate. A minute later I wished I hadn't.'

'Oh.'

'But—' the man cleared his throat and raised his voice '—I did leave thee to thyself once you turned ghost, 'tis true.'

G blinked.

'When I first turned spectre I was lonely, like you. There was no one about I could trust with my secret, no one but Sully. I knew he was a scoundrel but he wasn't all bad. Not evil back then, just selfish. Lettin' Sully get close to the Timecatcher was my second big mistake, and all because I was lonely. Now he's become crazed by the source, I think he's probably capable o' doin' any act o' badness to get what he wants. Once I realised what I'd done I swore to think o' nothin' but protectin' the Timecatcher from that moment on.

'I decided I'd only befriend folks, livin' or dead, if they could be a help with sealin' the portal and then only if I was satisfied that they were good, honest folk.

I watched thee for weeks after you died, hopin' you were one such, but you put me too much in mind o' Sully so I figured I'd keep thee at a distance.'

'Me, like Sully? That's not true! That's not fair!' G shouted indignantly.

Greenwood shrugged. 'You're selfish, quick-tempered, moody and unreliable, all things he is.'

G scowled and chewed his lip.

'These last few days I thought I saw a better side o' thee but then you let us all down by talkin' with Sully and makin' a secret o' it. Why are you here, Pooka-boy? Did he send thee?' Greenwood didn't sound angry, just tired.

'No.' G frowned.

But someone had sent him, someone had told him to find Greenwood. He screwed up his face and tried to remember. No use. The forest was spinning, he wished he could just throw up and be done with it.

'When is this?' he asked distractedly. 'What day are we in, anyway?'

Greenwood narrowed his eyes but answered. 'September. 13th September, 994, the day the ring appears.'

'Someone sent me in here,' G groaned. 'I can't remember who, but. Why can't I remember?'

'The Timecatcher is playin' with thee, Pooka-boy,' Greenwood said. 'It likes to confuse us what travel in it. It used to get the better o' me once; it don't give up its secrets easy.'

G lay down on the grass and curled up in a ball, clutching his stomach. Jessie's face swam inside his eyes.

Her mouth was opening and closing. What was she saying?

'Caw, caw.'

He opened his eyes and stared up at the branches sprawled above his head. A large, black bird was hopping about in the oak tree; as he watched, it snatched a butterfly from the air. Another 'catcher shade, caught in endless replay. 'Caw!' it said again and flew away.

G jumped to his feet. Greenwood was watching him with a weary expression that said, 'Go on, do your worst, Pooka-boy.'

'I remember now!' G said. 'Jessie sent me.' He looked at Greenwood desperately.

'Go on,' said the ghost. 'I'm listenin'.'

'I'm to tell you . . .' G faltered. That couldn't be right, could it? But it was. The pictures in his head were rearranging themselves now. He let it all settle in his mind for a moment till he was sure. He squared his shoulders and spoke.

'I'm here to warn you,' he said. 'Beware of the crow.'

** 36 **

'Here, Blot. Here, kitty-kitty.' Jessie pushed open the door to the studios. 'Come on, Blot. We need you. Master Greenwood needs you.'

If they could just find the Timecatcher cat, Jessie was sure they could persuade her to enter the vortex with a message.

Jason was more doubtful. 'Greenwood says she hates the Timecatcher. She hasn't been back in there since he brought her out a couple of hundred years ago. Even *he* can't entice her in.'

But they had agreed that she was their only hope of getting word to Greenwood and G. Jason had stayed in the office in case she turned up there, Nat had gone to check the kick-boxing studio and Jessie had left Duff with Jason and taken the artists' studios.

'Here, puss, here, kitty.' She half crouched as she ran, rubbing her fingers together as if she had food in her hand. 'Blot? Coaly-Cat?'

'She's in here.'

Jessie jumped. George McCabe's door was open. She went in. George was wiping his hands on a cloth. A black shadow was flickering about his ankles.

'Blot! Thank goodness.' Jessie knelt down on the floor and called the cat towards her, wanting to grab her, knowing that was no use. The ghost cat seemed reluctant to come, as if she already knew why Jessie was calling her. George unhooked his denim jacket from the back of the door.

'Are you leaving?' Jessie asked George, trying not to sound too eager.

'Yes.'

'Good! I mean—'

''S all right. The cat already told me to go. Seems to think I'm in danger of some sort.'

'Yes. You are. You've got to get out of here, right now.'

'Is it to do with the boy?' asked George, grabbing his keys and moving towards the door.

'In a way. He's—'

'Me?' said George.

'Yes.' Jessie looked up from Blot for a moment. 'How did you work it out?'

George blinked. 'It was his eyes. And the scar. I went through some old photos when I got home. I think Gran used to call me G when I was a kid. It's incredible but it all makes sense now – that feeling that something's missing, lost. I've been feeling sick all day; I suppose it's the shock.' He did look fairly green. 'What about him? G. Is he in danger too?'

Jessie nodded. 'We all are, but you and G most of all. I can't explain; there's no time.' She glanced at her watch. Two-forty. 'Please, go!'

He moved towards the door and Jessie made a sudden dive for Blot. The cat arched and spat before vanishing through the wall towards the back rooms. Jessie jumped

212

to her feet and ran out into the corridor after George. Together they dashed down the outside stairs. At the entrance gate he stopped.

'Will you be all right?' he asked. 'I can stay if you need help.'

'No!' Jessie literally pushed him out of the yard. 'You have to leave. Get away, now! That's what I need you to do.'

George nodded but he looked unhappy.

'GO!' Jessie shouted. He turned silently and walked out the gate. She dashed for the office.

'Blot?' she called as she opened the door. Jason shook his head.

'But she ran through the wall from the other side,' Jessie wailed.

'I haven't seen her.' Jason slumped in his chair. 'This is terrible, sitting here not able to *do* anything.' He kicked at the table leg.

Under the counter Duff jumped. He'd been dreaming of biscuits but something had just wafted through him and it tickled. He opened an eye; the scentless cat was walking away from him in a trickle of paws and tail. She glanced back at him and for a moment dog and cat eyed each other warily.

Biscuit, biscuit, thought Duff. He stood up and shook himself vigorously. He began to walk towards the stone steps. Biscuit, rat, rat, rat, rat, rat.

✳✳ 37 ✳✳

'$\mathcal{H}$e said he could get me back my life if I did something for him,' G continued. '"Nothing for nothing," he said. "You scratch my back and I'll scritch your itch."'

'He said that?' Greenwood asked sharply.

'Word for word,' G replied.

'Sounds like Sully, I've heard him say just such before.' Greenwood had listened to G's story with growing interest. 'He can take over the body o' animals, but not a man,' he stated firmly.

'How do you know that?' asked G.

'Because if he could do that, he'd 'a done it. He's comin' back to draw more power from the Timecatcher, much more, because that's what he wants – to take over the body o' a man, permanent-like.'

'Can you do it?'

'Take over an animal's body? No!' Greenwood looked shocked. ''Tis a terrible gift he's been given. A ghost is a ghost, a spirit without a body. That's how 'tis meant to be. And how it should be.' He pulled a face. 'The Timecatcher is full o' spectres, you say? 'Twould explain the buzzin' in my ears. Shish, now. I needs to think.'

Relief washed over G, relief at being believed. It felt good. The nausea was draining away and a tingling

214

sensation was taking its place. He suddenly felt strong and focused – and strangely compelled to look behind him.

Two shadowmen were approaching through the trees. One was juggling apples, the other was carrying something wrapped in a blanket.

'Master Greenwood, someone's coming,' he whispered.

Greenwood floated quickly to his side. ''Tis the ring thieves, has to be.'

They watched the shades as they came closer. They were dressed like street entertainers, colourful, with bells on their hats, bells that made no sound. The man with the apples was thin and lithe. He was juggling as if he hadn't a care in the world but his eyes were darting right and left and every few steps he spun in a circle to check the forest behind him. The podgy man carrying the bundle was sweating and yelping.

'It's hot, I swear, 'tis burning me,' he complained.

'Don't be daft, Donkey,' said his companion. 'Keep your voice down.'

'And 'tis getting heavier. There's no way we'll make it back to the horses with it. Me legs are starting to buckle.' And with that Donkey folded and sat in a heap.

'Ow, ow, ow, ow!' He bounced the bundle from knee to knee then tossed it off onto the grass in front of him. 'Thing's alive, or cursed, or somewhat, I swear, Tommo!' He tried to stick all ten fingers into his mouth at once.

'They expects us back with it by tomorrow. Himself will have our heads if we fail him,' hissed the juggler, stuffing the apples into his jerkin.

'Himself can carry it, then.'

'Here, give it me, you lazy oaf.' Tommo snatched at the abandoned bundle. He withdrew his hand just as quick. 'It bit me!' he exclaimed.

They stared at the thing in horror.

'What'll we do?' moaned Donkey. ''Tis full of bad magic. Himself can't expect us to carry off bad magic for him.'

'But we can't let Themselves get it back either, can we? 'Tis their magic, that's why Himself wants it. That's why he sent we pair of tricksters to spirit it away.'

'So as Themselves won't have it any more? Is that it?'

'Well, of course that's it. The less magic your enemy has makes your enemy lesser, you eejit, you.'

'Well, let's hide it, then no one has it, not Themselves, not Himself, not we, not me, so everybody's happy,' suggested Donkey eagerly.

'Except Themselves,' snorted Tommo. 'They'll never be happy without their precious ring. Here. I'll bet this oak is hollow.' He clambered up the oldest oak and disappeared into green. After several rustles he reappeared, head and arms swinging downwards. 'Sure enough, hollow 'tis,' he said. 'Hand us up the wretched thing, Donkey, old friend, quick as you can.'

Donkey approached the bundle cautiously. He circled it, making several half attempts to grab it, jibbering to himself. Just as Tommo was about to lose patience Donkey found his courage and launched the bundle into the air. The blanket fell away as it rose and gold glinted through the shadows as the Viking ring swung upwards towards the waiting Tommo. G and

Greenwood watched as the man tossed it quickly from hand to hand, swung himself upright and dropped it into the tree.

'There,' Tommo said, blowing on his palms. 'Done. Time to be off before Themselves work out who took their magic ring and slit our pretty throats for us.'

The ring thieves began to run. Greenwood had seen enough; he passed through the oak's outer skin into the hollow chamber inside. G watched Tommo and Donkey skedaddle through the trees for a moment. Did they get away? Had Himself punished them when they returned without their prize? He'd never know. He followed Greenwood into the hollow.

There it was. The Ring of Tomar, glowing on a bed of dead leaves. It had no stones in it, no rubies or sapphires, but it was breathtaking for all that. Three bands of gold wove together to form an open circle. At either end dogs' heads bared their teeth at each other, their flaring nostrils almost touching. Greenwood leaned down and passed his hands through it.

'It should give me more strength, maybe even enough to defeat Sully,' he said. For a moment he glowed so strongly that G had to shield his eyes with his arm. 'Go on, then, lad.' Greenwood pointed to the ring. 'See what it gives thee. We needs all the help we can get.'

G reached his hand towards the glittering surface. He could swear both pairs of dogs' eyes were suddenly trained on him; he even thought he saw a tongue flicker briefly between one set of golden teeth. He concentrated, just as the tae kwon do guy had taught him to. He brought all his focus to his fingers and brushed them over the surface of the ring.

'It's hot! Donkey was right,' he gasped. He ran his fingers along the dogs' heads and sparks ran up and down his arms. 'I can feel my skin! I can! I can feel the magic on my skin!' He looked at Greenwood in surprise.

And then the sensation was gone and the ring grew cold. It withdrew its brightness and the leaves that lay on the floor of the hollow began to rustle and shimmy towards it. It was as if the golden thing was pulling together a new blanket to hide itself in; within moments it was camouflaged so only a searching hand would find it.

Suddenly a scream filled the air. It reverberated around the tree like shards of glass. Jessie's voice. Jessie, screaming.

'Stop him, G! Stop him! Before it's too late!'

✶✶ 38 ✶✶

'**Y**ou best go back up to detectives' office quick-fast and see what 'tis.' Greenwood's face creased into a worried frown.

'Yes, sir!' G was about to leap up when a small black cloud tumbled into the tree and meowed.

'Blot!' Greenwood gathered his cat to him. 'Wait, lad.' He checked G in mid-jump. 'Let's see what she has to tell.'

The cat was shivering and G fidgeted anxiously as Greenwood stroked her fur, whispering quietly to her as she rubbed her face against his beard. He looked up at G suddenly. 'She's shown me a rat in the Timecatcher, a real one. Then she showed me Sully. She blurred the two into one. Sully's makin' his move.'

Greenwood stroked Blot with his other hand. 'What do we do, Blot? Stay and guard the ring or come with thee and chase the rat?'

Chase, chase! G prayed silently and crossed his fingers.

Greenwood looked at the cat for a moment but she wriggled and turned and sprang upwards in an inky surge.

'Chase!' Greenwood roared, springing upwards after her. Cat and ghost vanished into the vortex.

'Chase!' yelled G and shot after them. The

Timecatcher took hold of him and sucked him upwards in a twisting blur.

When G reached the edge of the void Blot was already leaping into another wave. G and Greenwood barely made it before the opening folded on itself. They spiralled downwards.

They landed back in the tree trunk in a riot of ghost arms, legs and tail. G just had time to take in how much smaller the hollow was and that it was winter, before he was overwhelmed by the same intense sense of magic he had felt from the Ring of Tomar.

The same, yet different. The power pulsing around the ring had been fierce and challenging; this magic was gentle, almost welcoming. He leaned down to check the earth at the base of the trunk but there was no sign of the ring amongst the dead leaves. Suddenly Blot was caterwauling and Greenwood was bellowing.

'Stop him! G, try and stop him!'

G turned to find a rat jumping towards his neck. It had something tiny in its mouth, clutched tightly between its front teeth. G grabbed at it but the rat sailed through his fingers, its eyes glittering. It hissed at G as it passed and seemed to draw its mouth back in a hideous clenched grin. Then it was gone, caught in the Timecatcher slipstream and the magic was draining away with it. Blot streaked by G and he rose to follow her, Greenwood at his side. The vortex swallowed them all and the trunk was dark and empty once again.

** 39 **

'We've got to head him off,' Greenwood's voice yelled close by G's ear. 'Whatever that rat's got between its teeth has strong magic, we mustn't let Sully take it through the portal.'

The rat was up ahead, clawing and racing along the waves and sinews of the vortex. Once or twice its tail was almost within G's reach, but now it was pulling away from them. Blot flowed from Greenwood's side, her small black shadow barely visible as she sped after Sully. She gained on the flying rodent, passed it and swung around on it, suddenly huge, teeth bared, spitting. The rat turned abruptly, almost losing its delicate grasp on the spinning wall, and scrabbled in a circle, as if confused.

'Let's see if I can haul thee out o' that rat, Sullivan Ellz'mede,' Greenwood snarled.

He raised his hands as he closed in on the rat, and concentrated. G held his breath. For a second the rat looked mesmerised and its little paws stopped moving. They all floated, rat, boy, man and cat, suspended inside the wave, for even it had slowed its constant course.

G gasped. Two transparent hands were emerging from the rat, fighting Greenwood's force, frantically pushing against the big ghost's pull. A head emerged, following the struggling arms; head and arms swelled up to normal human dimensions, snarling and wrestling against Greenwood's fierce draw. Black eyes glowed furiously in a mad face.

G drew back. The eyes turned on him.

'I'll have you, careless boy,' hissed Sully Ellz'mede, spittle flying from his lips. 'I'll have what you abandoned. Finders, keepers.' He gave the air another almighty push with his arms and Greenwood flew backwards as if he'd been struck. The contact was broken, Sully sank back into his animal host with a hideous cackle. 'Losers, weepers!' he hissed as he disappeared. The rat turned and the Timecatcher suddenly resumed its swirling.

'Master Greenwood!' G tried to fight the tide and get to the big ghost's side.

'I'm all right, lad; it's nothin'.' But he wasn't all right; G could see that. He was fading alarmingly, vanishing in front of G's eyes.

'Go, lad. Get after him. I've done drained all my power tryin' to cast him out o' rat's body. I'll be no more use. It's up to thee now. Remember, don't let that rat out o' Timecatcher. You can do it, Pooka-boy, I know you can.' Greenwood smiled and reached an arm towards G. His hand briefly ruffled G's fringe. 'Go, Ghostboy!'

G kicked against a wave and shot upwards. Glancing back over his shoulder he saw Greenwood, flailing in the current like a drowning man. The Timecatcher seemed to be swallowing him whole; he looked small and frail as he fell away into the void below. G gulped and turned his face upwards. The rat was far ahead, running for all it was worth. Sully's words echoed inside G's mind. Finders, keepers. Losers, weepers.

Why had Sully Ellz'mede said that to him?

What did he mean?

How on earth was he, G, going to stop Sully if a ghost as powerful as Greenwood couldn't?

His stomach did a flip and then another. And another. Blot had zig-zagged through him. Now she was flowing alongside him, keeping pace with his flight and staring at him intently.

'No, Blot,' G began urgently. 'You mustn't chase it out, Master Greenwood said—'

She crossed his path again and they wove together as they spiralled upwards. G's eyes widened. Pictures flashed inside his brain, driving out all thoughts of Greenwood and what he had said, all memory of Sully's strange threat. The boy laughed, and his laughter crashed and cavorted around the Timecatcher like a giddy puppy.

'Wo-ho!' he shouted. 'What a joke! You're on, Blot! Game on, Blot! Ready, steady, go!'

Boy and cat accelerate, gaining on the rat's tail. They chase it, faster, faster, ever closer to the portal, the portal to the Button Detective Agency. The portal to the outside world.

✳ 40 ✳

'Steady, Ratty!'

Sully fights the urge to take over, to smother Ratty's tiny presence altogether, to drive its little body Sully-solo towards the portal. 'Don't mind the pesky pussycat,' he soothes. 'She's not really there.'

Blasted Blot is close behind and the boy just behind her. But the cat can do nothing to stop Sully, she's just an irritating sprite. The boy, though, could use his hands to bat Ratty right out of the air. And if the rat once loses its tenuous hold on the gossamer nothingness that is the vortex wall, it will tumble, it and the magical thing in its teeth. Sully hasn't come this far to fail now.

'That was a near thing back there, Spikey-nose,' he muses. 'Old Greenwood nearly tore us apart, you and me, and what a wrench it would have been for Sully to leave his Ratty-boy. You'd have gone spinning to oblivion and I'd have had a time of it trying to wriggle out of grim Greenwood's grip. That would have made a right mess of my plans, Flea-brain, let me tell you.' Sully scowls and Ratty's eyes glaze over. 'Steady as she goes now, Ratty-boy. We're well shot of him!'

Ah, to just take over this stupid rat once and for all. Just push the silly animal right out of its own skin and steer this furball through the Timecatcher all on his

Sully-owny-o. And he could, too, if he wanted. He could take over Ratty right now, body and brain. With the Spark in his grasp he need only assert his will and Ratty's essence would be snuffed out in an instant. But, as things stand, he'll just have to put up with Whisker-face for another wee while.

'I can't negotiate this slippery surface without you and your animal instincts, Ratty-boy, more's the pity.' Sully sighs. 'I needs you to get me out of here and you needs me, so let's concentrate, Big-ears. Let's stay on message.'

'And, excepting the Greenwood moment,' Sully thinks, 'we are doing just fine. We have the precious Spark; the portal is in sight. Just a few more moments and we will be exiting the Timecatcher, dashing for the skirting boards, running through to Studio Six where the grown-up shell of that silly Ghostboy will be, painting his greyness onto canvas, grappling with the meaning of life inside his stupid half-a-head.

'Well, Georgy-Porgy-painter-pie, I'll change all that for you. We'll get out of this city and see the world. We can trick, rob and murder our way across Europe, and if we get caught I'll just body-hop to the next available eejit and leave you to take the consequences. I'll be in charge; you'll just be an annoying little tickle in the back of my mind. Like a conscience, har, har!' Sully guffaws at the idea and Ratty's whiskers wobble. 'No point in trying to make old Sully feel guilty, Georgy-boy; Sully doesn't do guilt. Biggest waste of time ever invented, is guilt. Giddy-up, Ratty.'

The portal is only a metre away but the rat is slowing

down, in fact he's positively skidding to a halt.

Dog!

A pungent smell of dog fills Ratty's brain and Sully feels fear flow through the animal from whisker to tail. Ratty wants to turn so badly that for a moment Sully loses the control he has been holding with such a careful, light touch. The rat turns quickly and there is the cat. No smell, but huge eyes, cruel and green. She's swelling in size, she's an alley cat then a lynx, now a panther!

Ratty turns again.

Dog breath, dog teeth, dog snarls. Ratty runs its little paws in circles.

Eyes see dog. Ears hear dog. Nose smells dog.

Turn.

Eyes see cat. Ears and nose, catless.

Definitely dog versus soundless, scentless cat.

Ratty twists away from the stink of dog, back into the Timecatcher.

'Oh, no, Ratty, my love, my darlin' boy, there's no going back now.' Sully takes control, he takes it all; the rat is pushed to the edge of its own brain. Sully turns back towards the dog. The girl's dog, his head sticking through the portal, blocking their way out, teeth bared.

'And where's that brat, Ghostboy?' Sully thinks. 'Can't see him anywhere. He's never gone and discovered who he is and run for his body after all these years? We'll make a race of it, har har!' Sully laughs. That chit of a ghost won't get in his way.

'Sadly, Ratty, this is where we part company, you and me. Only way out of here is through Doggy-doo up ahead, so I'll be leaving you and temporarily slumming it in dog-bones, har har har. The dog can take me to the painter just as well as my little rat-steed can. I know you don't mind, faithful Ratty. You'll lay down your grotty little life for old Sully and be proud to, won't you, Clickity-claws?'

The timing needs to be perfect, Sully knows, if he's going to take the Spark out of the Timecatcher with him. He and Ratty need to be almost in the dog's mouth when Sully switches hosts. It's the only way he can throw the precious magical thing as a rat and catch it again as a dog.

'So spit it out, Ratty, toss up our magical treasure, nice and high, allé-oop! There it goes, up, up. Well done and farewell, my Ratty-tatty. I'm leaping like an acrobat changing partners in mid-air, way-hey! Jump, flippety-boo. Allé-oop!'

Phew! Dog-breath!

Nearby someone is squealing, squealing in pain. A death-squeal.

'Oh, Ratty! Is that you? Why Ratty-boy, everything's gone black.'

✳✳ 41 ✳✳

'Come back, Duff, please come back,' Jessie begged. A tear rolled down her cheek. She couldn't see her hands. The pressure from the portal was squeezing them into numbness but she wasn't going to let go of Duff's collar and watch him tumble through the wall. Never.

They never had found Blot and there'd been no word from G. He'd gone into the Timecatcher hours ago. And, since Jessie had never told him where Greenwood was, he couldn't have found him and warned him about Sully. Now it seemed certain that G was in more danger from Sully than anyone else. G had a second chance at life and Sullivan Ellz'mede was going to snatch it from him. The thought of that evil ghost taking over George's body horrified Jessie.

Nearly all of Duff was inside the portal now. Jason and Nat were hanging onto Jess, all three of them were tugging with all their might but they couldn't budge the determined little dog. He was straining forwards and using the pull of the Timecatcher to counter their efforts. They had been stuck in a tug-of-war with him for at least ten minutes.

'It's the rat, it has to be,' Jason gasped through gritted teeth, jamming his feet against a step and sitting back with his arms locked around Jessie's waist. Nat had wrapped her arms around Jessie's ankles. 'What else would have attracted him to the portal? Let's try one big heave. One, two—'

'Shh! What's that noise?' Nat stared at the wall.

'It's the Timecatcher,' Jessie said. 'It whirrs.'

'No! Deep down, listen deeply down.' Nat put her head on one side, they all did. She was right. From far below them came a rumble. It rolled and gurgled upwards and the steps began to shake.

'What's happening?' Jason clutched Jessie tighter and she tightened her grip around Duff's collar till she could feel her nails digging into her palm.

'A-yarr-ah-oooo!' A high-pitched squeal pierced the bricks and rang piteously in their ears. Jessie shuddered.

'Duff?' Nat called, stricken. 'Duffer?'

Sudden they were all tumbling backwards.

Jessie lost her grip on Duff's collar as he burst back through the wall, leaping upwards as he came and snatching something out of the air. His jaws closed on it with a snap, he rolled on the buttons, found his paws and dashed under a desk with his prize.

The portal shimmered again briefly and Blot wafted through, eerie as black mist. She ignored Jessie and the detectives beached on the buttons in various ungainly poses, her eyes searching for dog. Once she located him she jumped onto a table and began to wash herself in the sun.

The wall opened once again and Greenwood emerged, looking so transparent as to almost not be there at all. He, too, scanned the room hurriedly.

'Where's the boy?' he asked urgently. 'And where's Sullivan Ellz'mede?'

Jason and Nat were scrambling to their feet, raining buttons as they rose. Jessie didn't move. From where she was she could just about see Duff in the shadows.

'What's Duff got in his mouth?' she asked, her voice shaking slightly.

'Not the rat! Please to say it's not the rat?' groaned Nat.

'The rat's dead.' Greenwood followed Jessie's eyes to where Duff was hiding. 'Thy dog done broke its neck for it; it fell away into the bottom o' Timecatcher.'

'Good dog, Duffer,' Nat exclaimed, reaching down under the desk to pat him.

'Don't touch him!' Greenwood shouted and Nat withdrew her hand quickly. He turned to Jessie. 'What is it, lass? You're lookin' at Duff strange-like; what is it you see?'

'His eyes. They're not Duff's eyes. Oh God, that horrible ghost's got Duff!' Jessie's face crumpled and Nat wrapped her arms around her and pulled her to her feet. They all stood and stared into the shadows. Jason stepped forwards; a low growl stopped him in his tracks.

The little dog scampered out into the centre of the room and stood up on his hind legs. He gazed straight at them, eyes that were not Duff's eyes challenging them to look away. He took three steps to his right, then three to the left. He turned full circle then dropped back down onto all fours.

''Tis Sullivan Ellz'mede,' said Greenwood quietly. 'And he's got a powerful magical thing between his teeth. Don't any of ye go near the dog or Sully'll jump from Duff to you.'

'We think he's after George McCabe,' Jessie said. 'But I got him to leave the building.'

'Who's that then?' Nat pointed out the window.

George McCabe was standing in the middle of the yard, arms folded, watching the windows anxiously.

'Oh no!' said Jason. 'Why's he still here?'

'He knows something's up. He must have stayed to see if we need help.' Jessie ran to the filing cabinet and jerked a drawer out, emptying the files onto the floor. 'Quick, Jason! Grab the other end.'

'What? Why?' Jason caught the other side of the drawer.

'Just do what I do,' Jessie yelled. Jason suddenly seemed to realise what she was up to. They ran towards Duff and upended the drawer over his head, trapping him underneath.

'Clever girl.' Jason nodded.

Nat looked puzzled.

'If Duff has the power source in his mouth, he and it are trapped under the drawer,' Jessie explained, 'and if Sully wants out he'll have to leave the power source in there with Duff.'

'Ha ha ha,' said a familiar voice and there, wafting out of the drawer, grinning at them, was G.

G.

Ghostboy.

Eyes dancing. Holding his belly. Laughing.

'You should see your faces! They're priceless, so they are!' he guffawed.

Greenwood tried to look angry but began to smile instead. 'You did it! You out-foxed that old fox Sully! Well, I'll be!'

Jessie freed Duff and gathered him into her arms.

Nat looked around the room. 'Then where is Sullivan Ellz'mede?'

'Moved on,' G and Greenwood answered together.

'Has to be,' said Greenwood.

'He tried to jump from the rat to Duff,' explained G. 'But he couldn't because I was already there. So he sort of bounced back into the rat.'

'And *you* killed the rat?' Jason raised his eyebrows; Nat pulled a face.

'Well, Duff did.' G's voice was full of admiration. 'I could feel how strong his instinct to kill it was. He was amazing. I just sort of sat back and let Duff do his stuff and he did it with one clean snap.'

'But surely Sully isn't dead, he just lost his host animal?' Jessie looked around nervously and tugged the irritated Duff closer. 'I mean, he's a ghost, he can't die twice.'

Greenwood shook his head. 'I was close enough to see some o' what happened. I sensed Sully for a wee second as he left the rat and then – nothin'. I thought 'twas because he had taken over Duff but now, well, now, I believe he has finally died with that rat o' his.' Greenwood seemed shocked, as if he couldn't quite believe his old adversary was gone. 'His spirit won't have survived a second death. He's moved on, at last.'

'Then what's that terribles noise?' Nat had to shout to make herself heard.

The rumbling from the Timecatcher had risen to a frightening roar. The room was shuddering, buttons were bouncing across the floor, a coffee cup crashed from a counter. The glass in the window frames was rattling and one pane cracked suddenly as if a stone had hit it. Jason caught his laptop as it tumbled off his desk. Duff broke free of Jessie's grasp and ran into a corner. Jessie fought to stand up as the floor shifted beneath her feet.

'Sully must be coming back,' she cried.

'No! He's gone,' Greenwood insisted. ''Tis the Timecatcher. The magic is awake!'

'Duff has the magical thing that Sully stole from the tree,' G yelled.

'The Ring of Tomar?' Jason, Jessie and Nat chorused.

Greenwood shook his head. 'Don't know what it is, but it has huge power and it doesn't belong out here.' He pointed at the wall above the steps. They all stared in horror. A huge hole had appeared and a bright swirling mass was pouring into the room. 'Quick!' Greenwood bellowed. 'We've got to get that thing out o' hound's mouth before he swallows it.'

Jessie turned to grab Duff. The very air seemed to be fighting her as she dragged him out from his corner. The mass flowing into the room was pushing everything ahead of it and Nat was struggling towards the counter trying to reach the biscuit tin. They all watched as she tugged the lid slowly open and turned the tin upside-down. Biscuits fell away from the tin sideways. Duff leapt to snatch one and as he opened his jaws something tiny fell out. Jason caught it, held it up quickly for them all to see, then fought his way to the portal and tossed it at the wall. There was a jolt and everyone, even Greenwood and G, juddered and shot backwards. From the floor Jessie watched as the shimmering mass on the steps seemed to go into reverse and spiral into the wall. The bricks shot into place and the roaring slowly receded. The room ceased to shake and everything became quiet again.

The only sound was Duff, happily crunching on his chocolate biscuit.

✳✴ 42 ✴✳

'*A* bone, I think it was a shard of bone,' Jason said when he finally had his hands on a mug of newly brewed coffee.

'Or a tiny finger or toe bone, maybe.' Nat nodded.

Nat was perched on a chair, knees drawn up to her chin. Jessie held Duff close and tried not to shake. It was over, Sully was gone. The portal to the Timecatcher was still open but the danger had passed, for this year at least. Greenwood smiled and faded away to rest. G paced up and down, grinning from ear to ear, kicking buttons, high as a kite.

'Duff certainly liked it, whatever it was,' G said. 'He wanted to gnaw it something rotten but it stopped him. The thing just kind of said no, so Duff kept rolling it on his tongue instead. He was brilliant. He was way cool.'

'And how about you?' Jason smiled. 'You did really well in there, G.'

'Oh, it was all Blot's idea. I couldn't have done it without her and Duff. It was a team thing.' He stroked Blot just as he had seen Greenwood do many times. The murky shade responded by rubbing her head against his cheek, then striding away into the filing cabinet where she nonchalantly slotted herself in between W and XYZ and disappeared.

'She showed me a picture of Duff at the portal, then she showed me another where she kinda merged me into him. She had to do it twice before I copped on.' His eyes filled with wonder. 'Imagine, I could have been jumping in and out of rats and cats and stuff all this time and I didn't know.'

'Maybe, maybe not.' Jason looked thoughtful. 'You said you actually touched the Ring of Tomar when you were in the tree with Greenwood. You may just have gained the power to jump at that moment, we'll never know. Came in very handy anyway, eh?'

'Why can't Greenwood do it, then? How come I got the same gift as Sully?' G frowned. He didn't notice Jess and Nat exchange glances; he was too busy pacing.

'I've been thinking about that.' Jason cleared his throat. 'Greenwood was an unusually strong man in life; the Timecatcher gave him back strength, supernatural strength. Sully was a slightly different story.'

'What do you mean?' G stopped pacing.

'Well, we know Sully jumped out of his body before he was fully dead,' Jason said carefully. 'I think that means his spirit, the part of him that jumped, never really knew death. The Timecatcher gave him the power to reconnect with life, to go on jumping in and out of bodies. So Sully decided to make the ultimate jump to a human host – George McCabe.'

'Narls. I thought it was Narls Cunningham he was after.' G glanced questioningly at Jessie. She chewed her lip and half-buried her face in Duff's fur.

'We think he switched to George when he realised that George was an easier target,' Jason continued.

'George nearly died once, you see. *Did* die, in fact. In an accident. Here, in the mill.'

G stared at Jason then looked out the window at Painterman, who was now standing anxiously at the bottom of the back stairs.

'Only he was revived, later, in the ambulance,' Jason said gently.

G's eyes were huge. He slowly shook his head.

'But part of him was gone,' Jason said. 'Part of him had stayed here in the mill. Part of him had turned ghost.'

'No!' G was shaking his head vigorously from side to side. 'No! Rashers McCabe was one of the gang. He ran off and left me, just like all the rest. It was me died in the mill, me.' He looked from face to face. He stopped at Jessie's.

'It's a lie!' he said. 'Jason's making it up. It's a big fat lie!' He kicked a pile of buttons and they hailed through the air. 'I'm not like Sully, I'm not! I'm dead. I'm totally, completely dead.'

'George has your scar, G,' Jessie said. 'He lives with his gran on Manor Street. He is trying to paint because everyone tells him that's what he most wanted to do when he was a kid. Only he can't remember being a kid. He lost all his memories in the accident.'

G pulled his shoulders up around his ears. His hands dug into his jeans pockets; his fringe fell down over his eyes.

'I think that's why you've never been able to leave the mill,' said Jason. 'As long as George is out there still alive, your hold on death is actually quite thin. So you've been trapped here, where you "died".' Jason smiled encouragingly. 'You should be pleased. You have another chance at life, G. It's there, waiting for you.'

They all looked out at George.

'NO!' G was furious, his fists were clenched, his mouth was distorted. 'Shut up! Shut up about George McCabe. He's not me. I'm twelve, he's old. He's dull. He's the most boring eejit I ever met.'

'G—' but Jessie didn't get any further. He swiped at what was left of the coffee mugs and they hit walls and floor, cracking and splattering as they went. He rose up above their heads and made for the door, then changed his mind. He flew to the steps and paused at the portal. He threw another angry scowl at them all. The bricks parted, the Timecatcher beamed out its yellow light, the wall closed again and he was gone.

✳✳ 43 ✳✳

*A*fter school next day, when Jessie reached the Button Detective Agency door, Duff decided to stay out on the landing in the sun and not even a chocolate biscuit would entice him inside.

'Pull up a seat, Jessie,' Nat called over her shoulder as Jess came in. 'The portal closes tonight so I'm doing exit countings to find out roughly how many ghosts end up stuck in there.' Nat was sitting in the corner beside the steps watching the portal. Jessie bumped the other office chair over the buttons to join her.

'Ah! Another two,' Nat said, waving at a couple of old ladies wafting through the wall, giggling and hiccuping. 'That makes seven hundred and eighty-eight ghosts out so far.'

'How many went in yesterday?'

'At least two thousand. We couldn't be totally accurate in our entry figures, there were so many, so fast. At least they're coming out in small groups.'

'But G?' Jessie asked anxiously. 'Have you seen him since yesterday?'

'The boy-ghost came out this morning, very grumpy, muttering about raggy boys and a beetroot concert and looking a little green. The Timecatcher seems to make him travel-sick, probably because he's not fully ghost.

239

Anyway, Master Greenwood took him in hand. He insisted they go back in and witness what really happened the day of G's accident. When they came back out G was very quiet and, after a bit, he vanished. Greenwood says we must leave him to think about it.'

Nat shrugged, then stiffened. She looked closely at the shiny bulldog clip at the top of her clipboard. She put her finger to her lips to warn Jessie to say nothing, waggling her finger slightly over her right shoulder. Jessie tried not to be obvious and stole a peek from the corner of her eye. Sure enough, there was G, very faintly visible, lurking in the shadows. Listening.

'Two, four, six,' Nat counted, in an extra loud voice.

An entire family had blown out of the wall, looking dizzy and tired. 'May we come again, Daddy?' asked the smallest child as they drifted away through the window.

'Looks like the Timecatcher might become a ghost holiday destination,' Jessie said. 'Just as well it only opens once every seven years.'

'That may change,' said Greenwood, suddenly materialising beside them. He gazed gloomily at the portal. 'What happened yesterday may alter pattern o' things a bit. No knowin' how.'

Jason came through from the back room. 'We now know we have at least two objects of great power in the Timecatcher – the Ring of Tomar and a tiny bone of some sort. Both of them seem capable of causing great destruction if they're moved out of the Timecatcher.'

They all looked at the wall, remembering the shocking sight of the vortex spiralling out into the room the day before.

'I've been checking around this morning,' Jason said. 'It seems every watch and clock in the mill stopped dead at three o'clock yesterday. Luckily the disturbance registered as a mini tremor on the Richter scale and was reported as such on the news, so no one else in this building is aware they were in particular danger.' He turned to Greenwood. 'We've managed to avoid disaster this time, Master Greenwood. Me and Nat will keep working on this with you; we'll do whatever it takes to protect the Timecatcher and seal the portal.'

'Me too,' said Jessie.

Greenwood smiled wearily and brought his huge hands up to his face to rub his eyes. 'That's good but right now the Timecatcher is full o' ghosts and we've no way o' makin' them come out. *And* that wee magic shard o' bone is exposed for all to see and probably lies in the wrong day altogether.'

Nat stared at the wall for a moment. 'I have idea,' she announced. She turned to face them all with a smile. 'Buttons! They will make great camouflage!'

Greenwood looked puzzled.

'Camouflage?' Jason and Jessie said it together and laughed. Jessie heard G, in his corner, smother a snort.

'Camouflage!' Nat nodded firmly. 'They will swirl and fall and hide the piece of bone, wherever it has fallen, yez?'

She grabbed the sweeping brush and started to herd buttons towards the steps. Jason grabbed the office bin, emptied the rubbish onto his desk and began to scoop buttons with it; Jessie grabbed the dustpan. G gave up his hiding place and joined in, picking up handfuls of buttons and slinging them at the portal. Nat began to sing.

'Red and yellow and pink and green, purples and orange and blue,' she warbled.

Jason laughed and began to sing along with the little nursery song. Jessie and G joined in; even Greenwood sang as they shovelled and slung. Soon the wall had swallowed thousands of the little coloured discs and the office floor, buried in buttons for years, began to emerge into the sunlight.

Moments later ghosts started to dribble up through the portal, disgruntled and confused, muttering and grumping about being tickled by hailstones. The dribble became a rush, Jason quickly resumed the exit poll and before long the ghost-tally was up to two thousand, two hundred and forty-seven and counting. Greenwood entered the Timecatcher to see what was happening and G went with him. They emerged a few minutes later, smiling.

'The buttons whirl down and the spectres swirl up,' Greenwood said happily. 'The sensation o' buttons flyin' through thee is a mite uncomfortable; I think we may yet flush 'em all out.'

'And it's so cool in there.' G laughed. 'All the colours spinning! It *is* like we made a rainbow.'

✳✶ 44 ✳✶

G was on the back stairs, lazily threading himself in and out the steps like an eel.

'So, boy-ghost!' Nat came out onto the landing where Jessie was sitting watching him. 'What is it to be? Life or half-life? Motorbikes or walking through walls for ever and ever?' She eyed him curiously.

'Dunno.' G shrugged. 'Painterman is dull as a ditch. I don't want to be him if that's all I can be.'

Jessie said nothing, just frowned.

'I think George is sweet and kind and rather good-looking,' Nat announced. 'And he is moving to Galway next week so you better make your mind up fast or your chance, it will be gone.'

'Galway?' Jessie exclaimed. She saw alarm in G's eyes.

'Yez!' Nat nodded. 'He told Jason about it yesterday when Jason went down to the yard to tell him everything was okay. He says he is moving on and if G wants to stay stuck here, it is up to him.' She leaned down and ruffled Duff's fur. 'I hope you do the right thing, G. For you and for George.' She straightened up, went back into the office and closed the door.

Jessie looked at G.

'Don't you start,' he snapped.

She shrugged.

'He's rubbish at painting,' G growled.

Jessie nodded.

'And he hasn't got a motorbike.'

'No. But you could get one, if you were him.'

'But what if I just become him? What if I get all swallowed up and become George Super Dull, the dreariest being on the planet?' He simultaneously pulled a superhero pose and a dopey face.

Jessie laughed. 'That's not possible, you eejit. It'll be half-you, half-him. I'm sure it will.'

'Or I could just stay all me,' said G. 'There's good stuff about being a ghost. I can fly. I can walk through walls. And I can be twelve for ever and ever.'

'Aren't you kinda sick of being twelve?' Jessie asked. 'And weren't you tired of being alone all the time?'

'I'm not alone now. I want things to stay just like this.' He folded his arms and pulled his head down between his shoulders.

'I wish things could stay the same for always too, and I'll miss you if you go away,' Jessie said softly. 'But I won't be twelve forever.'

Neither of them spoke for a while. They watched a small cloud drift across the sky.

'I'm scared, Jessie.' G hid his face. 'I don't want to change.'

'But you do want to be alive again?' she encouraged.

'I dunno. I – I – what if I don't know how any more?'

There was a low woof and they both looked at Duff, sitting a few steps below them, back firmly turned on the boy.

'He's still mad at me, I suppose.' G fiddled with his fringe.

'Well, yeah! What do you expect?' Jessie laughed.

Footsteps clattered into the yard below them and Duff trotted down the stairs. A familiar figure in black leaned down and the dog rolled over happily for a scratch. G evaporated beside Jessie, but she could hear him breathing, tensed beside her.

'He likes you, Duff does,' she called down to George.

George smiled up at her. 'Probably smells my dog off my jeans.'

'You have a dog?'

'Yeah. He keeps Gran company during the day when I'm here.' He gave Duff one more scratch and crossed to the front stairs. When he reached the door at the top he looked over at Jessie. Only he wasn't actually looking at her, more squinting to her left. Exactly where G was sitting, invisible. The man hesitated in the doorway.

'Tell your friend, when he's ready, I'm here,' he said and closed the door behind himself.

G reappeared beside Jess. 'Humph!' he said.

'So what's it like in the Timecatcher?' Jessie asked.

G laughed. 'You'd love it. It's way cool.'

'But what did you see? Who are the raggy boys? What's a beetroot concert? I want to know every little detail.' Jessie leaned back against the railings and hugged her knees.

G grinned. 'Where do I start?' he said.

'At the beginning,' she replied.

It was six-thirty by the time G had finished telling Jessie all his Timecatcher adventures.

'Wow! I wish I could have been there.' She sighed.

'Me too,' G said.

'I've got to go, G.' Jessie stood up. 'Me and Mam are going for a picnic tea in the park. I promised her.'

G pulled a face and nodded.

Duff woofed impatiently in the yard where he'd been dozing in the shade.

'He's in a hurry,' G said.

'I'll stay another little bit if you want.' Jess checked her watch with a slight frown.

'Nah. 'S okay. Go on. Yer late.' He gave a half grin.

'Yeah. I'd better. Only, she's a bit lonely, my mam. She's got no friends around here yet.' She started down the stairs at a run.

'Jess?'

'Yeah?' She looked up at him from the yard.

'We're friends, you and me, right?'

'Of course.' She waved and Duff ran ahead of her into the shadows under the archway.

'Always?' he asked.

'Always.' She grinned at him but there was a catch in her voice. She waved one more time, ran under the arch and was gone.

'Bye, Jessie,' he said quietly and wafted into a wall.

In Studio Six, Painterman was waving a brush in front of a blank canvas. G watched in silence for a while, then lost patience.

'Get on with it, you eejit, you,' he growled.

George didn't turn. He went on staring at the canvas as if he expected a set of instructions to appear on it at any moment.

'I don't know where to start.' George shrugged. 'Everyone says I wanted to be an artist when I was a kid, so I've tried. But I guess that was a you–bit, not a me–bit.'

'You're moving to Galway,' G said accusingly.

'Yeah, I need a change,' George said. 'I want to move on. I've always felt stuck, like something was holding me here. It all makes sense now. But it's time to go. You can come with me if you want. 'S up to you.'

'What's our dog called?' G asked gruffly.

'Curly.'

'He going to Galway?'

'Of course.' George put down the paintbrush.

'Start with an umber wash,' G suggested grumpily.

'Right.' George put some paint onto a plate, mixed it with water and picked the brush back up.

'Bigger,' said G. 'That one.' He came closer and pointed. 'And you'll need some yellow ochre as well.'

George changed brushes and squeezed the golden paint out beside the brown.

'Now paint,' G ordered.

George's hand hovered in the air, brush centimetres from the canvas.

'Oh, for heaven's sake.' G floated closer.

George held out the brush to him without ever looking over his shoulder.

G moved forward. He reached his ghost fingers out to take the brush. He hesitated. He could just take it.

He knew he could do it now, he didn't need Painterman. But ... but ... he chewed on his lip.

Now or never.

He put his hand inside George McCabe's hand, inside his own hand and drew on his skin like half-familiar overalls.

G's spirit slipped inside bone.

Real breath crashed through him.

His own heartbeat exploded in his ears. Ba-boom. Ba-boom.

He rolled the paintbrush between real fingers.

He moved towards the canvas and swept the brush across the surface in one fluid movement.

He flicked on the CD player.

'One, two, three, faw,' G shouted in unison with the guitarist.

Then he began to laugh. His laughter echoed around the room and the colours on the canvas began to dance.